MY
YEAR
OF
LOVE

OTHER WORKS IN DALKEY ARCHIVE PRESS'S
SWISS LITERATURE SERIES

Isle of the Dead
Gerhard Meier

Why the Child is Cooking in the Polenta
Aglaja Veteranyi

With the Animals
Noëlle Revaz

Walaschek's Dream
Giovanni Orelli

The Shadow of Memory
Bernard Comment

Modern and Contemporary Swiss Poetry: An Anthology
Luzius Keller, ed.

The Ring
Elisabeth Horem

MY YEAR OF LOVE

PAUL NIZON

TRANSLATED BY JEAN M. SNOOK

DALKEY ARCHIVE PRESS
CHAMPAIGN / LONDON / DUBLIN

Original edition: *Das Jahr der Liebe*, Suhrkamp Verlag, 1981
© Paul Nizon / Actes Sud, 1985.
Translation copyright © 2013 by Jean M. Snook

Library of Congress Cataloging-in-Publication Data

Nizon, Paul.
[Jahr der Liebe. English]
My year of love / Paul Nizon ; Translated by Jean M. Snook. -- First Edition.
pages cm
Edition originale: Das Jahr der Liebe, Suhrkamp Verlag, 1981.
ISBN 978-1-56478-844-3 (pbk. : alk. paper)
I. Title.
PT2674.I9J3513 2013
833'.9'14--dc23
2013007170

Partially funded by a grant from the Illinois Arts Council, a state agency

The publication of this book was supported by grants from the Swiss Arts Council
Pro Helvetia and the Office for Culture of the Canton of Bern/SWISSLOS

swiss arts council
prohelvetia

SWISSLOS
Culture
Canton de Berne

illinois
ARTS
Council
AN AGENCY OF
THE STATE OF ILLINOIS

The author wishes to thank the Pro Helvetia foundation of Switzerland for
emergency assistance during work on this book.

The translator wishes to thank Edith Killey of Toronto for her detailed explanation
of the unique Paris street-cleaning system; the author Paul Nizon for approving
a slightly expanded description of that street-cleaning system in the translation;
and Neil Bishop, Professor of French at Memorial University, for stylistic
improvements to the English translation of the "Révélation du Destin."

www.dalkeyarchive.com

Cover: design and composition by Mikhail Iliatov

Printed on permanent/durable acid-free paper

THIS DREAM, I'M WRITING IT DOWN NOW in the afternoon, more or less for practice, here in my boxroom, while the dove man starts *nagging* his missus again, whining, his whining getting louder and softer until her shrill, raspy voice cuts him short, making it clear who's in charge; and while the small child screams, but it's not a scream, the sound is more strained and nasal, a matter of life and death, of self-defense with nothing but this baby sound that verges on suffocation, on respiratory failure; while from a lower window the stubborn, orgiastic stamping of a rock band continues relentlessly, from farther away there are normal voices and laughter, and then the monotonous, robotic, artificial speech of TV dialogue with sound effects in the background

while all that's been going on, it's become late afternoon, but since we're an hour ahead here with daylight savings time, it's just a little after four, I'm writing down this dream that I'm in Rome, right at the place where, in my ever-recurring DREAM ROME, I come to that gateway or that narrow passageway where it "goes around a corner into paradise or into supreme bliss," down a long, long, sloping flight of stairs—but it's difficult to find the gateway to that corner that leads to supreme bliss

but I was there two hours ago and ran into Livia from my scholarship year, she's older too now, by the more-or-less seventeen years that have passed, you can see it, and yet she's the same freckled redhead, apparently she's lived in Naples all these intervening years, she's the daughter of a professor, I remember now, and so there she is, in the company of several others in the same age bracket, and despite that, they're all still students, all still on scholarships, I'm the only one who isn't anymore, I happen to come across them where they're drinking tea or having a picnic behind ruins overgrown with vegetation, with hardy evergreen ivy, thorny, pretty, I'm not particularly welcome, but they let me stay, so I sit down with them on this bench for idle *Deutschrömer*, German artists and writers who came to Rome in the nineteenth century, it's almost as if I'm invisible, or not quite as real as the others, I'm with them but they're by themselves and take no notice of me

and there at my feet, under the table, is a cat who starts playing with my shoe, eventually turning over onto her back and hitting at it playfully with her paws, but also really wildly, and then she grips the shoe or my foot firmly with her teeth, and although I keep wanting to shake her off, I notice that I can't, I'd have to grab her by the fur at the scruff of her neck and fling her away, or push her away forcefully with my foot, and I finally turn to my company on this stone bench to ask them for help, *they* should get rid of this cat for me, but they don't react at all, and only now do I notice that I'm with a party of the blessed—or am I the dead one among the living—they don't react, or they act as if I didn't exist

and then all of us, these overage students or *Deutschrömer* and I, ride down a road in a sort of handcart, we're going to the institute, I presume, and I'm between the shafts, but can't steer properly anymore, it's going too fast and will end up crashing

and later, at last, this Livia, who's gotten rather heavyset and really tall, she was always a beanstalk who thought herself sylphlike and behaved accordingly, this Livia turns to me now, frankly bored, and asks if I still work as a journalist, and I reply, almost indignantly, that I haven't been a journalist now in a long time, for really quite some time now I've been a full-time professional author writing books, yes, she had heard that, but also that I wasn't making a go of it, she says, and as I energetically protest, she's already turning toward someone else again, and what's a dream like that supposed to mean, but I woke up in a good mood to the noise and voices from the courtyard, to the accumulated sounds of human life in France, of Parisian life that volubly invades my courtyard, this droning, talking, this roar of life here that never stops. *And life there will never end*, I once wrote and meant THE OTHER LAND, the sought-for or promised land—of inexhaustible, eternal life and now, in my room, I'm thinking of Dorothée, that's the name my girlfriend goes by in Madame Julie's *maison de rendez-vous*, I had chosen her from the selection of girls who were paraded quickly past in Madame Julie's grandiose salon, and I had chosen well, because it isn't easy to decide so quickly when so many of them, one after another, step up to you at the bar and smile at you as they shake your hand and Madame Julie calls out their respective names, and while you're trying to form an impression and you want to remember a name, which is of course an alias, the next one is already coming along—but I had made up my mind without hesitation, although I would have considered two or three of the others as well

then when I was upstairs I looked at this one more closely, because I wasn't entirely sure if she was the one I had meant, but she looked pretty upstairs too, very pretty, in our plush bedchamber, her short, dyed blonde hair framed a pert French girl's face, in which two brown eyes glistened wonderfully, eyes that laughed pleasantly from the start, offering friendly companionship, and her mouth was seductive, full, not too large, protruding, *as if slightly swollen from a bee sting*, I read that once and found it wonderfully put, and I noticed right away that her hair was dyed blonde, her natural hair color is dark, my God is she beautiful when she stands there naked now, having slipped the close-fitting black evening gown over her head, and having nothing else on underneath, she is beautiful, I think, her slender body has wonderfully smooth curves, it's magnificent how her stomach and bottom and thigh swell outward, not too much, but with a seductive effect, one would like to drink such a body, *you have a delicious body, easily digestible* says the Robber in Robert Walser's novel to a maidservant, I think, that's put so damned nicely, it's awkward and de-eroticizing, whereas *this* body, for all its slenderness, says woman, which is a rare impression to get from such a young girl, and her breasts are so provocatively curved, firm and full and turned slightly upward, one would like to drink someone like that, to drain her like a clamshell, and now, quite unembarrassed, she's washing herself on the bidet, and I'm standing in the doorway and talking with her, and then, when we're in the big wide French bed, everything belongs to me, all our limbs are now intertwined in that wonderful show of confidence that exists only in love, you can see from my pubic hair that I'm not really blonde, she says, and she candidly—if that's the right word—tells me all kinds of things about herself

Dorothée used to work in a clothing store, she was in sales, but she also took care of purchasing, she said, and when the store expanded and added an upper story where she had full responsibility, all by herself, she thought she would get a pay raise, she wasn't even earning two thousand, more like one thousand, she said, and the boss refused, she quit in a fit of anger, she hadn't even worked there a year, and now she works for Madame Julie, she has a boyfriend, he's twenty-eight and writes music for chansonniers, he's even written for Sardou, never heard of him, I say. What, but you must listen to the radio and watch TV, Sardou, you'd certainly know him

and then in bed this whole rubbing against each other and stroking and kissing and more and more and this entire girl, this woman in the girl called Dorothée, when she lies there like that afterward, she puts her hands over her breast and stomach, one up over her breast, one down over her stomach, but not actually as a gesture of self-protection, because after all, down below she's bare and relaxed and lying there with her legs spread, bare and relaxed, what are you doing with your hands, that's pretty, I say, but why that. That, she says, is how I always lie, when I'm asleep, or rather, when I wake up, I see myself lying like that. It's a little like a small child's posture when she caresses herself, possibly, but I don't understand anything about that

that really *is* love, I say to myself, simply because it's all there, everything that belongs to real love, from the kissing to the inability to stop and every form of embrace and then the real bit of loving, accompanied by a lot of panting and sighing and little screams and puffing by both of us, and as we do so we *do* love each other, when we desire each other and our limbs and skin are mutually attracted to each other, because if we didn't we wouldn't be able to let ourselves go and

and now, early on a Sunday morning, I'm sitting at this little table, Place Clichy, in September, a bright, clear morning, and bitingly cold, and I see Rue d'Amsterdam with its own magnificent sky reflected in the street canal, not much traffic yet, and we're sitting in the enclosed sunroom on the café patio, Beat and I, Beat in his Burberry, he can wear that, he's tall and slim, even if he's really broad in the shoulders, so that the English coat hangs correctly and can even hang loosely as he walks, Beat with his Watusi skull and his dark, searching, and slightly ironic eyes behind his steel-rimmed glasses, the two of us are sitting there, he's a visitor, I'm the resident, but what does resident mean in such a city, what would be better is: I'm the one who's vanishing, the fly, the louse, the atom here, the one who has escaped, and I say, I'm so happy, Beat, that I've managed to do it, to finally make the break and to move here, don't you think, it's like starting life anew, at almost fifty, don't you think, I say, and I tell him what the others are saying, that my whole official departure, the bureaucratic process of canceling my registration with the local police and having my emigration officially sanctioned, none of it was really necessary, those were just gestures, and look at all the disadvantages they brought, such as the loss of my health insurance and old-age pension and survivor benefits, all of which were obvious drawbacks, they say, I tell Beat. It's like a marriage certificate, it's the creation of an unambiguous predicament, it's the inverse dilemma, he says, and that makes a difference, quite clearly. He means the difference between being someone on holiday who does return to his homeland after all, even if he departs repeatedly for longer or shorter sojourns abroad. It's a burning of bridges, it's a real risk, says my dear friend Beat, and now I think I could welcome him here and feed

him, I'm on the other shore, free, *footloose and fancy free*, I once cop-
ied down longingly

at first, Beat's eyes were sleepily stuck together, his skin doughy
and pale, his complexion that of someone who hasn't had enough
sleep, you must have been partying last night, Beat. He was, even if
I only find out about it from him bit by bit.

I'm sitting at this little table as if I were in the New World, like an
emigrant, I feel like an outlaw now and am grateful to my wet nurse,
to this great old city, and also somewhat proud that she's turning herself out so magnificently on this gleaming cold September morning,
Place Clichy, and now, just to strut about a bit, I cross the square to
buy some cigarettes. I wrote two letters late in the night, still wildly
elated, while listening to a jazz program on the radio, and now that
I've mailed them at the reception desk in Beat's posh hotel, I can give
him my undivided attention. We'll go out for lunch soon, Beat, don't
eat too much now, because I want to make off with him to the Por-
tuguese canteen I just discovered recently, almost as far out as Porte
de Clignancourt. To pass the time, we take quite a roundabout route
across Place des Abbesses, then down Boulevard Rochechouart, and
even into the Arab streets that are so disreputable, supposedly, but so
wonderfully alive, and, yes, almost unnatural, because to our way of
thinking they're so completely sealed off, they have names like Rue
de la Goutte d'Or and Rue de Chartres, and we seem to be right in
the Orient. Then along Boulevard Barbès with its busy Sunday market, and further along Boulevard Ornano. Escaped, escaped, a voice
and a small voice in me rejoice as we walk along

yes, how the other voice rejoiced, the clarinet of this young man,
probably a student. He was playing with two banjo players and a
bassist in front of the Printemps department store, just a while ago,
it was last week, and a considerable crowd stayed and stayed there on
the widened sidewalk in front of the store. The people couldn't tear
themselves away, young and old, whatever skin color, even children,

and now and then someone would walk forward to throw a coin into the instrument case on the ground, that was so moving, these individual people stepping forward, going up to the stage to say thank you, it wasn't at all as if they were "just passing by," because the people who made the contributions stepped right back again into the ring of listeners, each of them was giving thanks, alone—like going up to an altar with an obolus, like laying a wreath, bowing down, it was a public show of feeling. These individuals who stepped out from the crowd to go up to the four young musicians, some of them were shy, among them very old people, others were cautious, as if not to disturb anyone, but all of them went up to show something, but what? Gratitude, approval, solidarity?

It was infectious, it was above all the clarinet, it grew out of this very young guy like an elongated mouth, a trunk, that seemed to be grown together with, connected with his puffed out left cheek, and the kid was all music, a shrill, jubilant, wonderfully sustained clarinet sound, vibrating through and through, carrying, carrying us away, the whole young man was sound, indignation and complaint and consolation, the melodies hung almost visibly out of his mouth, out of his body, sometimes he squatted down, as if waiting for his three friends and inspiring them, his instrument turned toward them, a *singular* invitation and inspiration, and the banjo-boys and the short fat one on the bass played noticeably better

how that rang out, complained, rejoiced, tugged and tugged, tugged at our feelings. Sometimes, when the banjos led, or the bass had a solo part, he sat down on the protruding base of the department store, small and bent forward, tapping his right foot to the beat and very quietly, almost murmuring, playing an accompanying melody, an accompaniment to the entrances of the others, until he leapt up again for his own entry and the air and our hearts burst. No one could tear himself away, and there was no contact at all between the musicians and the listeners except for this deep contact conveyed by the music later on, inside the department store, as I was looking for a purse for my mother, a purse I thought of taking her as a present for her approaching birthday, her seventy-ninth, I still heard the music, but I wasn't sure if I was really hearing it or if it had merged with me, entered me to such an extent that I now heard it playing, singing, complaining and triumphing in me

and I felt only love for all the others who had stood in the circle outside with me that morning

my mother, I see her stalking stiffly to the door with short steps, she's gotten short and bent. It's her new apartment, this senior's apartment, modern and cool, somehow this apartment makes a gray impression because it's so purely functional, but maybe that's just because of the gray wall-to-wall carpet and the relative darkness—although an entire glass wall looks out on the patio at the back, the living room is only bright when there is really brilliant sunshine; the building is located below Kornhaus Bridge, and even though it's surrounded by a magnificent circle of trees, it's not light here. And Mother keeps the apartment clean and sterile, as if it didn't belong to her, as if she had only been put here to keep it clean, to keep things in order, in the bathroom and the kitchen with all their built-in cupboards and compartments, there's nothing lying around that would indicate the apartment was occupied, and yes, I see fear in my mother's face and hear it in what she says, fear of making a noise, fear of noises of any kind. And a correspondingly exaggerated, downright subservient show of friendliness to the outside, to the other occupants of this seniors' complex, I don't know, is she intimidated, in some way humiliated. When she comes running with little steps, so stiff and bent, and opens the door to this one-room apartment that seems empty despite all the furniture, as empty as a garage, in fact, even her surprise, her pleasure is or seems feigned, I'm not sure if she fully realizes that I've made the trip here now to visit her or if she thinks I'm always here; that would be terrible, if she were in such a mental state, or would it be liberating? Given that she's gotten gray as a mouse, is no longer in service, has been pushed aside

how nice that you've come, you're the only ray of light in my life, she says, and the tears are already coming to her eyes: you know, I think all the time now of passing away, if only I could pass away . . . But what are you thinking of, are you having difficulties, don't you have any coffee, I ask brightly, and now she makes a pot of coffee, it really smells or tastes strange, I say, unfortunately, and regret it right away, because she's already starting to act defiant or angry, and she stalks into the kitchen to show me the tin, Nescafé, my God, and it comes pre-ground in buckets, is that old age, I think, because my mother used to be really proud of her coffee, and now she brings out a bowl of cookies that have almost turned to dust already, if not to plaster, she puts it down beside the dreadful dried flowers and the bowl of fruit with the oranges and apples that are already shriveled

and we sit by this wall of windows at the pretty little triangular table with the Biedermeier base and the Biedermeier chairs, and I notice right away that she herself never sits here, you're still not taking your meals here, Mother, I ask, because everything seems so unused, and she admits that she's accustomed to having her breakfast and even the main meal of the day at the kitchen counter, this built-in counter, you know, then I can clear everything away again in a minute and do the dishes and not waste any time. But you *have* time, Mommy, I say, why don't you make yourself at home here, you have all the time in the world. No, she says, already acting defensive, as a cautious and preventative measure, and soon she'll start to accuse me of things and get annoyed with me: no, what makes you think that. Every morning I get up at six, then I clean the kitchen and the apartment, after I've made the bed, your mother has always worked, all too much, as it happens, and now I notice that an odd, musty smell pervades the apartment, and I catch myself thinking that she won't be able to bathe very extensively, with the open sores on her legs, her legs have always had slightly open, oozing sores, and in the evening or the morning she has always treated them with ointment and wrapped them with elastic bandages, no, with those legs she'll hardly be using the hypermodern shower, and why should she shower, I think, and now, on her beautiful head, that's gotten somewhat smaller, I detect something like a horn under her full hair tied back in a bun, it seems to me that her forehead is sporting something slightly like a horn, or is it just because I find her so obstinate and narrow-minded that this image occurs to me and flits before my eyes

I sit down on the bed, couch would be a better word for it, and can't think of a thing to say. In the stone-gray room I sit across from my silent Mom, take some of the dusty cookies, drink the lukewarm, tasteless, instant Nescafé out of the beautiful old English china cups, black with a gold pattern, and outside there's this unused patio with no flowers or plants, and beyond the patio a lawn with tall old trees, and above them stretch the struts and arches of the old cast-iron bridge that makes everything so dark and dismal that it's best to switch a light on. I turn on the radio

Writing practice is what I call this note taking, my daily task, I could also have said: warming up. Warming up, so as not to get rusty, to keep myself going. Or do I do it solely to evade this terrible freedom or emptiness? I'm in Paris, but I'm in this room that's narrow as a box, and time is passing. I'm waiting. Waiting for something to move. Like the hawk that circles above a gray landscape, and when something moves, it plummets down and tries to grab the moving thing with its talons. It has to happen fast, as fast as I can possibly think, in a nosedive, as it were, or else I wouldn't start writing at all. I make up my mind to do something and get started at it. I begin the same way an athlete does, he sizes up the course, then summons all his strength so he can jump the hurdles effortlessly and brilliantly. I make up my mind to write about my little nugget of an event or an experience or even something I've just imagined and type it up fast. I cast it out, and, sizzling, it solidifies in the matrix of language. I take a look at it. It's like the New Year's Eve custom of pouring lead into cold water to tell one's fortune for the coming year, I pour myself in small depictions into the emptiness of my day, in my boxroom, in this gigantic Paris piled up around me, where "life" is hiding or has lost its way. Like the athlete, I race to the typewriter and fling it out, if possible in a single sentence, no matter what. No matter? No, I do have to be attracted by something. A flash of lightning? At most in the sense of a fish shooting out of the water. That's beautiful, the jumping of fish, a flash of silver in the air and it's over again immediately. Or I write about something I've picked up on the street, and I think about it at home, about what I've picked up, or even just about the jumping of the fish that I thought about during my walk, about this flash of lightning, while I putter around in the apartment, or fiddle with things in the kitchen to put it off, anything rather than beginning, but then I sit down, I throw myself at the typewriter and onto the paper. If I didn't behave that way, I wouldn't begin at all.

Fear? Fear, in this boxroom that looks out on the courtyard.

The courtyard. It shows me cracked, dirty white walls, and windows. Down below, separated by iron fences, carefully subdivided sections of the courtyard, cement gardens with plants in pots, rusting bicycles, garbage. Up above, a many-sided cutout of the sky. Across from me: the old dove man.

I hear the hoarse screaming of the baby. And the trilling, rejoicing, chirping of birds in cages. Songbirds. Their singing ranges from a mosquito-like humming through enticing single whistles, then a series of single whistles, to cooing, to fluting, and finally to a very bright tremolo.

And the hoarse screaming of the baby has this desperate straining to it, one senses the effort of will and the helplessness of the tiny red-faced body lying on its back, kicking, it has no other defense than just this straining sound that is finally suffocated in sobs.

And just now the dove man's nagging caused a big scene again with his missus, escalating until it verged on violence, then she quickly shut the window. He's the bellyacher, it doesn't take much to set him off, and he keeps at it until she gets into high gear herself and gives as good as she gets, answering in that Frenchwoman's voice that you know from *chansons*, that petticoat voice. He tries to drown her out, but you sense right away that she'll keep the upper hand.

He sits across from me. I see into his room on the opposite side of the inner courtyard, and he can see me at my table, in fact, he can see me better, because he lives one floor higher and can look down at me. Since I've been coming here, since I've been living here, for years, I've seen him sitting sideways at the open window, or behind the half-open window, and now and then behind the pulled curtain, an old man with gray, steel-wool hair, in a gray wool shirt, square head, a cigarette between his lips, he sits there and plays his game with the doves. For a long time, I didn't understand what it was about, this constant strewing of birdfeed, a handful on the window ledge, later he takes it away again and strews it on the adjacent window ledge, and when the doves come, he shoos them away with his hand or a little stick, reaching out from behind the cover of his window, ambushing them. For a long time I couldn't make any sense of this absurd maneuver between attraction and expulsion. Then I figured it out. He only wants to feed the one dove, his favorite dove; for her, he places the little piles of seeds or crumbs carefully on the window ledge, and also moves them from ledge to ledge, everything is intended for her, he follows her with the food, he watches over it so that she alone gets to enjoy his gifts, while the others, the ones he hits at—they must go.

He sits at his window from early to late, day in, day out, year after year, sometimes he reads, sometimes he has a cap, a beret on his head, I don't know if he's an invalid, he can stand up without any trouble. He does his thing with the doves, that's his only activity, aside from the extremely loud exchanges with his wife; whom I recently saw in her bra, now that it's really warm, their window is wide open in the afternoons, and that's when I saw her for the first time far back in the dark recesses of their room. Sometimes she hangs up their laundry diagonally across the room, from the free-standing clothes closet to another piece of furniture out of my line of sight, then their room is full of sopping-wet laundry, and they dine beneath the sky of their room decked out in this manner. Of course he has his television on all day long, maybe that explains the sideways position, his typical way of sitting, he wants to keep both the thieving doves and the television screen in view. We have never yet even nodded at each other, although we sometimes stare into each other's eyes for minutes at a time. We keep tabs on each other, I'd like to know what he thinks of me.

The beating of the doves' wings is also part of the stew that brews in this courtyard cauldron. Sometimes it sounds like clapping, while at other times, when they've been frightened by something and fly up in a flock, like whirring. Not to forget their cooing. Often a wingbeat sounds like the crack of a whip. Incidentally, in among the common doves, there's a turtledove that bills and coos every hour of the day, and through the night too.

The windows facing the courtyard show me many of my neighbors, mostly black, young couples, some with many children; the women, and even the tiniest little girls, sport Afro hairstyles, with strands of hair, big and small, twisted into antennae.

The yelling of the dove man, the shrill voice of his missus, their marital duet. Then silence. And the movement of the sunlight across the whitish walls of the inner courtyard, its slight or severe darkening due to clouds I cannot see, and then the sunbeams licking the walls again, a source of happiness.

This waiting, a laying siege to myself. And then I sleep again, in the middle of the day, preferably in the afternoon, and with no bad conscience at all. Sleeping is part of working, I say. Forgetting. Forgetting what's going on and accumulating up there in my braincase, in my head. Letting it subside. I lie down on the wide bed, eager to dream, while the old dove man pursues his doves or is glued to his television, and while the small child crows, I lie down, a still life of limbs, legs apart, and let the afternoon cover me gently like a soft eiderdown. After that, it takes a little while before I'm fully awake again. First I rinse out my mouth with my favorite mouthwash, "Eau de Botot," then I rummage around in my correspondence, but preferably in the kitchen, I do housework with ecstatic pedantry, as if I could make up for something with this perfection, could simulate real work. I dawdle until something starts to stir in my mind or my spirit, maybe even starts to take shape, something that may have been prepared while I slept starts to surface, to form, tips of icebergs jut into my consciousness, I cling to them while I continue rummaging around. I don't let the tips or angles out of my sight. Waiting

This waiting, for example in the Metro, together with other people who are waiting on the long, narrow, finely wrought bench. Seen from this bench, the subway tunnel seems spacious with a low-vaulted ceiling; and its white, bathroom-like tiles are glistening—an upside-down bathtub. It's like standing at the shore, then there's a streaming and thundering as if a torrent has just been let loose, and you sit and watch the train emerge from the black void and arrive and position itself with all its brightly illuminated windows in front of the curved walls with their huge advertisements, it's like sitting on a beach or a riverbank. When it departs, after a brief stop, and after the beeping that announces the automatic closing of the doors, it is once again the wide, empty hall, the bathtub, and we can look far down onto the riverbed, empty except for the train tracks, a shaft. And waiting again, together with others who are sleeping on the benches, tramps who are sleeping off their intoxication, their time, leisure time that goes on forever.

And against the backdrop of the glistening walls, the people on the far shore look exceptionally well dressed, better than I've ever seen, and there are many nonwhite people among them, Africans, Asians, Caribbeans, French from the overseas regions; and very old people, who have to live on these implausibly small incomes, and very young people, students, tourists; and one person without shoes, with felt boot-liners on his feet, he keeps running back and forth and then conspicuously inconspicuously going and standing somewhere else, beside the vending machines with gum and nuts, and then again in front of a group of tourists. And all of them share the same fate, together on the shore, the waiting ones in this beautifully illuminated underworld, or on their way together on a little trip to the end of a short night that leads into day again, elsewhere in the city. Then it's an entering into the day with amazement, with new eyes: coming up onto an avenue, a boulevard teeming with daily life, or else a deserted street, stonily dismissed by its tall buildings. The blind journey, and the sighted surfacing. Sometimes, after arduous hours spent trying to work, when I finally went out and through the turnstile and ran down the stairs that led to my line, I had been so moved down there in the brightly shimmering tunnel, so moved by the sight of the waiting people that the tears came to my eyes, why, why on earth? Because I was among my fellow human beings and noticed that I liked them, all of them without exception? Or simply because there were some people there and I was still there, although I had been *away* at home in my solitary confinement, now I was there, ready to ride the rails.

I love the Metro. I'm always running *away* when I walk along the street heading for the next station, and as soon as I begin the descent, when I feel the impact of the warm, musty, stale updraft that assaults me and grabs hold of me, forcing me to brace myself against it and clutch at my fluttering coattails, when I pass the few strangers who are climbing up and into the daylight, strangers I would like to greet and do greet secretly, as soon as I begin the descent I always start to feel fine again, and unburdened.

Down below, I always have this feeling of solidarity, because I'm so busy hurrying along with the other people, walking along with them, that I can completely forget myself, can get completely free of myself. Even more than in the stations, I feel it in the long, reverberating corridors I have to pass through when transferring from one line to another. It's cool here, just bare walls, and I'm running into these surging crowds, masses, armies, until I see nothing but legs, legs that are crossing my path, pant legs, stockinged legs, and all kinds of shoes, platform shoes, stilettos and espadrilles, sneakers, boots. A forest of legs, scissor legs. And sometimes notes and scraps of melodies wander around in these underground passageways, they come from musicians, there are always musicians down there who have their plate or violin case or some other thing, even just a scrap of paper, lying in front of them to appeal to the charity of the passersby. I know a few of them. There's an old man barely clinging to life, he's as inconspicuous as a cipher disintegrating and blotting itself out of its own accord, and since he has no instrument, he plays old records on a gramophone. There are always accordion players there, frequently also young people with sheet music playing Vivaldi or some other old master on their violins or flutes in all seriousness. But most of all, I love the saxophone players who tootle their jazz into their gleaming probosces, it follows me for a long time through the long corridors, notes, scraps of notes, the souls of notes that have gone astray. Sometimes I hear two things at once, the sonorous babbling sound of a wind player and an accordion player working his bellows to squeeze out a musette.

I'm sitting here in my boxroom in Paris, "like in the city of Paris," people used to say at our place in Bern when I was small, which means, they said, "one after the other, like in the city of Paris," and of course I said it too, without knowing what it meant, but somebody explained to me later, that the expression refers to the order of the courses of a meal, first the hors d'oeuvres, then the main course, then salad, then cheese, fruit, perhaps something sweet, then coffee, one after the other, like in the city of Paris, I'm in Paris but I'm in this boxroom that looks out on the courtyard and the dove man. Sometimes I hate him, so he must remind me of myself, how else could my hatred be explained? My friend Lemm, he's a physician, also somewhat of a psychotherapist, and for me he's a sort of guru, in any case my friend Lemm once said to me, if you get that worked up about someone else for no apparent reason, when there's been no cause for conflict, but you're constantly thinking about him, concerning yourself with him seemingly needlessly, compulsively, without being able to drop the subject, so that he dominates your thoughts and your conversations with yourself, although you see no real reason for it, if you swear at him, curse him, said Lemm, that means that you're worked up about one of your own weaknesses, a weakness you don't want to admit, that you want to hide from yourself; the other person simply made your own weakness visible to you, like holding up a placard, a roaming self-reproach. Back then, it was Florian B. who irritated me. He lived in the same building. So it's possible that my hatred for the dove man, who sits at the window all day and does nothing, is self-hatred? I see this guy ad nauseum, I see the courtyard, and then I see this or that when I go out, go out on little errands, just this morning I made a quick trip down to Rue Rodier to buy a new typewriter ribbon and have a few pages photocopied at Madame Tribolet's, I took the bus, not the Metro, I set little goals for myself to get some exercise, just as one has to exercise a horse, or a car, the latter on account of the battery, and I set little goals for myself in exactly the same way, otherwise I wouldn't get out at all, and in doing so I see the streets, different views of the city, stretches of the sky, I experience it as I have before, and I could write about it, but where should I begin? Write about *life*. Then, after that, I was at the seamstress's, another such pretext, I took her my old jacket that's already covered with leather patches hiding the worn-through parts, I'd like to keep the jacket, we've been together for such a long time, but the seamstress, an Arab with bleached hair, told me the latest abrasions or worn-through parts would have to be repaired by invisible mending, if at all, but that costs a fortune, so she suggested that she turn the jacket for me, the jacket is blue outside and plaid inside, the inside is still in good condition. I could write about that too. Is that life? So where the hell is life? As I'm thinking about that, it occurs to me that I've been intending for a long time to write about Wertmüller in Zürich, to date, I've bought four typewriters from him, beautiful old machines, prewar models, but of a quality, that is, precision, that can't be matched by even the most modern machines, he says. When he talks about one of them, he contends that it deserves to be called the Rolls Royce of typewriters, so I definitely will have to write about Wertmüller someday. "Wertmüller, Office Machines, I'm not in the store right now," is what his answering machine says, he's never in the store, he's in a bar, but he's the last competent typewriter mechanic, I fear, an artist in his trade, I note that I'm always expecting him to die and fear the impending loss.

I'm sitting in my boxroom, and when I sit this way for a long time and stare at the dove man, that obnoxious person, in fact when I stare into the courtyard at all I get scared. Because after all, there's a huge city piled up around me, a city full of life, and time is passing. And I'm sitting at my table like the old dove man at his window, and life is running through me too, in the form of thoughts, feelings, fears, tiny rays of hope, feelings of sadness, running, it's running down. So I seat myself at the typewriter and get down to work on something from my own gray, lukewarm timestream, something that I put aside for myself during the day, stuck into my vest pocket, as it were, then I warm up for it as I would for a long jump, or better: hurdles, I concentrate on the starting line and fling myself at the typewriter, blindly, in one leap, one sentence, and my only thought is that I have to land on my feet. If I succeed, then I'm not just seeing the fish now like a flash of silver, but am pulling it to shore. Pulling it to shore? Am I the fish? Have I pulled a piece of MYSELF to shore? or some bit, a small piece of life? Something solid, a finished product, almost a day's work already—whereas in the case of the old dove man, if *he* should ask himself what he's accomplished in a day, it would be at most feeding his dove.

Write something or pull it to shore, that is, put it on paper, otherwise you'll get sick in this freedom, it's unlimited, I would never have believed that freedom could be a form of captivity, freedom can be like a primeval forest or like the ocean, you can drown in it or disappear and never, never ever find your way out again. How can I make it to shore in this freedom, or how can I enjoy it? I have to parcel it out for myself, plant something in it, cultivate it, I have to change it, at least a little, into an occupation, freedom is a bottomless abyss when it presents itself in this totalitarian form.

How I longed for freedom when I was still in Zürich. It always seemed to me as if I'd been robbed of the day. And it was always evening, it's already evening, I said to myself. First I had to take the dog out for a walk. I waited impatiently as he was busy sniffing everything, these detours to the left and right, these embarrassingly exact analyses of the ground, with his nose on a spot on the sidewalk that was invisible to me, a scent mark, oh the damned beast, I thought, impatiently shifting from one foot to the other, and sometimes I tugged at the leash, shouted at him, and he looked up at me as if he were looking over the top of a pair of glasses, both reproaching me and asking my indulgence. But he stubbornly braced himself with all fours against my tugging, against the leash, against me, and I thought, what a burden, I was tied to the dog that pulled me all over the place, which is why I inwardly cursed him, and then I felt bad about doing so, he doesn't have it easy with me, if only I hadn't saddled myself with a dog, I thought. And people walked briskly across the street, and I stood there and waited for my dog to finally stop his sniffing and snuffling and do his business. I was always torn between scolding, grumbling, the gestures of a lord and master, guilt, and love. Dearest dog, I thought, when he got sick once and the people at the animal hospital feared he wouldn't pull through, my dearest dog, I thought, and was about to cry, I was already choking back the tears, and I got all emotional thinking about his grumpy behavior when late, very late at night, he had rolled himself up into a ball, his nose deep in the bushy hair of his tail, like a fox. Then he was unapproachable, and if I called him, if I called out to him, to tease him, then, without moving, he just breathed out grumpily, almost growling, to signal his displeasure. And I regretted scolding him and pictured our walks when man and dog were going along the street side by side, in step with each other for once, and he would suddenly stop and just sniff the air, he savors the wind with his snout, his nostrils, he purses his flews and filters the air through his teeth, virtually biting it, getting the news by tasting things, the incredible things of a world I have no sense of. But, then again, when I'm in a hurry, on the way to meet someone, and I think it's important not to come too late, I brusquely tell him to get a move on and I curse canine behavior, and at that very moment, at the most inopportune time, he comes running up to me with a branch, presenting it to me like a transverse flute held in his teeth, head high, tail up with pride, the *entire* dog an invitation to play. Now of all times, I think, and I don't know if I should laugh or cry, you always bring on this diabolical inner conflict in me, and later, as we walk along, he shoves his moist snout against my hand, as if to say, "we two are pals, right," and I feel indebted to him, he's a noble dog, say my friends. *Flen* is a lord, said Karel, who used to share my studio and was always drunk.

In Zürich, I longed for freedom. My day was always fully booked and a waste of time, I wriggled in a net of commitments, by evening I felt chopped to bits, the day was already spent, and I longed for freedom, for the possibility of considering something and pursuing it at my leisure, no matter what it was. Move out, away from everything, I can't thrive here, move out, transplant myself, I thought, that's the only solution.

And even before that, when I was in Bern and an assistant in the museum, I had finished my university education, *that* burden, and then I went into the museum day in, day out, my small office was right next to the entranceway, a door the size of a barn door, which could hardly be moved. My small office had bars over the window, inside it smelled like a grotto, damp, and I sat at my desk working on some inventory cards, what was this stuff to me, and outside the day was going by, a day with speeding streets and strolling people, and I was sitting over this monotonous work. It smelled of corpses in that museum, of mummies, revoltingly sweet, and every morning my dear Herr Oleg came along, Herr Oleg was over seventy, a Russian emigrant, an agronomic engineer, he had served under the tsar and later under the Bolshevists and had traveled through all of Russia on important, very important jobs, but he had finally fled, and now he was working here as an engineering draftsman in the prehistoric department. For health reasons, he started work at nine, not at eight like the rest of us, and he always dropped in to see me before starting his work at the drawing table. He folded his face into a kind smile, and his eyes looked at me with faint amusement, well, young Dr., that's how he liked to address me, I was twenty-seven, but looked twenty; and then he told me a story, at every opportunity he thought of a story. He took a metal case out of his pocket and put a cigarette in his holder, not a whole cigarette, one third of a cigarette, a stub, he cut his cigarettes in three at home and filled his case with these miniature cigarettes. It wasn't so much a way of economizing as a means of protecting his health, a ruse, he should have stopped smoking long ago. It was in the capital city of *Pschrrssssk*, as he prounounced it . . . he began, and then came the story of the beautiful couple, head over heels in love and recently married. They had moved to this city one day and all eyes were on them, a couple like in the fairy tales, I lit a cigarette for myself too and sat lounging in my swivel chair, the couple was the talk of the town, obviously there wasn't much going on in that provincial capital, everybody knew everybody else, and so people were happy, just because it kept the gossip going, when there was a newcomer. The couple would soon have been forgotten if another character hadn't turned up, an ugly guy, *hair like licked by*

27

a cow, said my dear Herr Oleg, and his body bent like Paganini's, *a real son of devil*, he said, but this guy then started to get interested in the young married woman, that is, he pursued the woman, which of course could not remain hidden from the people in the small city. Well, he didn't have any say there, we thought, the young married couple had eyes only for each other, everything was new to them and beautiful, being married, everything. But one day, well, what excitement in the city, the young woman had vanished, and indeed with Paganini, if you can believe it, because, says my dear Herr Oleg, *moral is of story: Men love with eyes, but women love with ears: if you put violin in women's ears, then they become soft as wax for your hands to grasp.* The devil's son had courted her with words of such virtuosity that she couldn't resist, in any case she had gone missing along with him. Now I'll be going, said Herr Oleg and withdrew, at the door he made as if to bow *and wish you four and twenty pleasures.* And I bent over my inventory cards or over the annual report while the sun wandered uncertainly past the barred window.

I was in this dark building, built in the style of the old castles, and I wanted to get out. I looked out through the barred window of my ridiculous office that was squeezed into a side tower. Through the trees, I saw passersby on their afternoon walks, I felt the sky brighten and darken, and everything that was going on outside seemed beguiling to me: people out for walks along the edge of the forest in the nearby zoo, perhaps old people leaning on something or someone and stopping to rest again and again, turning toward each other to finish talking about some small matter with all due emphasis; that looks odd, that method of moving along, old ladies standing still on a leaf-strewn walkway in the afternoon. Then they go on a few steps, stop a while, arm in arm, only to stop again. And as background noise I imagined the dry plop plop of tennis balls being hit, I saw the smooth-trodden red earth of the tennis courts behind chain-link fences. In all this time the old people have only progressed a few small meters on their walk, and now they turn their necks to look behind them, because a large bird has sailed overhead, over the forest path, a crow? And the smell of the forest comes wafting over, and something is rustling in the bushes, small birds, nothing more. I wished I were there, I would overtake the two old ladies with long strides, I would bathe my head in the still afternoon air. The scents of the forest and the earth and the slightly rotten smell of leaves. And in this tiny tower room, where I already had to turn the light on, I bent over the boring annual report again. Soon it would be evening, but closing time wouldn't seem like a release to me—together with everyone else at the streetcar stop I would declare the day lost, and I hadn't even noticed what the weather was like. I hadn't even been able to experience the weather. I tore the day off the calendar.

The two old ladies—or perhaps it's one old lady, definitely well-to-do and charming, already walking with a stoop, while the other one is younger? the nurse, companion? a younger relative? and when they turn to one another like that under the canopy of leaves on the forest path, it looks from a distance like a conspiracy; or the lady is saying: that's how it is, my dear, and I also wanted to mention . . .

The old dove man has had his hair cut or trimmed, I saw that when he leaned out the open window to hit at a dove with that ridiculous cane, the cane is bent at the front, a metal rod with a hook, a crook, the two-faced shepherd. He's wearing gray woolen things, the cigarette dangling from his lips. Now he looks like a convict or like some old man from an asylum. His trimmed gray hair over the gray wool knitted vest . . . He really is an inmate, someone out of a home, a madhouse, or perhaps an overseer, a bad man. Always hitting at doves that, to his mind, are unauthorized, and therefore punishable. Now and then he leans out the window to yell something at someone in the courtyard, something that begins with MERDE, of course. When he's sitting down, he sits sideways, so he can keep an eye on the television and the doves and *me*. He obviously has no problem with freedom, with free time. In the mornings, before turning on the television, he reads the newspaper, he seldom has anything in his hands that looks like a book. A disgusting character, I often think I can see an expression of sneering superiority or malicious gloating on his face. I think: this dirty swine, this bastard, this totally superfluous scoundrel, vermin, ORDURE. He pollutes the air with his presence and ruins my mood with his roaring. Has he been pensioned off early? He can't be all that old yet. An invalid? But I see no sign of any physical disability. What he's been doing now for years—or for decades?—is not only ridiculous, it's scandalous. Feeding doves and swiping at them, snapping at his wife, bawling out people in the courtyard. I don't understand why he gets me so worked up, I still don't understand it. When he takes his seat by the open window and lets his slimy, spiteful, almost lecherous eyes wander in my direction, that is, recently he's been looking past me or pretending to look past me: then I always feel as if a snail has crawled over me. I think he wants me to watch him, that he craves my attention.

Recently he disappeared for a few days. It was the first time he'd ever failed to appear. For a while his window was wide open, showing the room as a yawning black hole. His one favorite dove perched on the window ledge for a good while, then I saw it—I didn't imagine it—hop into the room and disappear from view. Later it was standing at the window again, looking baffled, I thought. Two or three of the other doves also stood for some time on the adjacent window ledge, looking helpless and bewildered outside the window that had in the meantime acquired a billowing curtain. No raucous voice, no nastiness, not a sound. I wondered if the old dove man had died, I was preoccupied with that question, I was totally absorbed by the thought, downright hypnotized by the empty window. Actually, I should have been relieved, but the opposite was the case, I was concerned. If only he hasn't died and gone away forever, I heard myself think, anything but that. I had grown accustomed to the guy. A life without the dove man—I would feel impoverished. Let him come back with all his damned yelling, I murmured inaudibly, just let him come back, please don't take him away.

The next evening, the old woman was suddenly back at the window. I waited. She came and went, several times. There was something uncanny about these appearances at the yawning black window. Then she stood there and started yelling at someone—at whom? there was no one to be seen anywhere, far as I could tell—with a shrillness that verged on madness. You filth, she screamed, you shit, son of a bitch, bastard, for years now I've been cleaning your ass, so cut the playacting, I see you, she screamed. With whom is she talking, I wondered, horrified, could it be that she was addressing the old dove man, that now that he's died and she's alone she's letting him have it, or rather letting his ghost have it, somewhere down there in the courtyard?

But the next day he was back again, looking downright jovial he assumed his usual sideways position at the window, with that crafty, derisive, supercilious expression, so self-satisfied that I found it almost obscene. And I thought: oh you bastard, if only you'd stayed away forever, I thought that and said that and felt relieved that I'd been spared that ordeal *one more time*.

You dirty swine, I whispered each time I passed Florian's apartment on the stairs, I couldn't wrench myself away from the topic of Florian, it was like a compulsion.

I lived in a room in the Zürich *Altstadt*, the old part of the city dating back to medieval times. The room could have been called a studio, one of its walls had four windows that overlooked the *Altstadt* roofs, and if I stood at the window, I could glimpse a bit of the river between the roofs and the buildings. But I seldom stood at the window, I sat with my back to this wall of windows, at an enormous table, an ironing table from the past century, it was a veritable expanse of a table, its surface polished bright by all the ironing, but now strewn with papers and obscured by them, it was a time when I was doing a lot of work. In contrast to the Romantic view, I felt anything but romantic, and in no mood to be charmed by the *Altstadt*,

I paid no attention to my surroundings, I was in a race against time with my writing, a race against the hours, I often wrote through half the night. That's why I sat with my back to the windows, I ignored them, I wanted to write myself free, to write myself out of there and into the open, I was obsessed, enraged, tugging at my chains.

This Florian Bündner lived below me. He too had a large table, a rustic table with bulbous struts, a dark-stained Renaissance table. The entire surface of this piece of furniture was laden with piles of newspapers, books, documents, and junk mail, the books and papers and newspapers were stacked up into tall, swaying towers. If he had invited someone over, which was all too frequently the case, then he had to transplant one or two towers onto another table, but since the second table, which was also rustic, if somewhat smaller, already held several towers of files, the transplantation was a tricky undertaking. Florian was something like a teacher. Actually, he was a runaway student, one day he had broken off his study of German language and literature as taught by Professor Emil Staiger, I don't know what semester he was in or the cause of his departure, from that point on he seemed to occupy himself entirely with private projects, and in order to finance himself and these projects, he taught a few German classes as an assistant teacher at a commercial school that could only be interested in this subject and in literature, if at all, insofar as the prospective merchants needed to be able to write a business letter that was grammatically correct, with the periods and commas in the right places. As for literature, those courses were offered at best for the purposes of providing a bit of conversational trivia. Yes, it was at this school that my fellow tenant taught, he performed his duties in an extravagant, persuasive, and, as people said, revolutionary style that was captivating and inflammatory and flew in the face of his contract, which is why the students seemed to love this teacher, he stood out from the other instructors by virtue of his effusive independence and his eloquence.

The German classes were Florian's only job, and they provided him with an income that, although modest, was obviously adequate. He was not at all interested in doing any more work, because he wanted to keep himself inwardly free, available, after all, not for nothing had he distanced himself from the treadmill of the university.

He got home from the school late in the morning, but since his room was so crammed full with reading material, he couldn't think of staying there or of beginning to do anything, so he left right away again and went to a café, where he entered with a newspaper, journal, or paperback under his arm and gave the impression of being absorbed in the printed matter. But his absorption didn't last long. If he saw someone he knew, he couldn't help inviting that person to his table. He gave the impression of being a jovial intellectual, due to the books and papers he always carried around with him and always postponed reading to a later date, since his innate sociability interfered with his reading and prevented him above all from reading anything to the end, which is why he loaded his books, newspapers, treatises or illustrated catalogues onto those tall, swaying towers.

My housemate's problem was that he simply couldn't clean up, he would have had to separate the important things from the unimportant things and put his things into meticulous order, but this task seemed hopeless, a task for Hercules, but not for Florian, which is why he understandably kept putting it off, so it wasn't surprising that hardly had he come home and unloaded his things than he sought to get away, out into the street, or a café, or he invited people in. Florian was a passionate host, he always had several bottles of wine in stock, vodka too, and besides, he liked to cook, his standard dish was small thin slices of meat cooked in sauce and served with rice, a quick meal he could conjure up at any time, and as his guests drank more and more wine, the decrepit old building resounded with Florian's daily and nightly banquets, I could share in it all upstairs in my studio at my ironing table.

The building consisted mainly of a dark stairwell like a cow's stomach that swallowed anyone coming in. Once the newcomer began to climb the creaking, squeaking wooden stairs, the impression of being in something's entrails intensified, it smelled of all kinds of excretion, of kitchen odors, apartment odors, of sorrow and sweat. When I crept up the stairs, I could not only smell my fellow lodgers, but also see them right before my eyes, their whole physical beings, their frailty, their good habits or their bad. There were no apartment doors, just room doors that all led directly into the stairwell. Florian's kitchen door was always open, and from it poured a torrent of kitchen odors and the stink of sweat.

No sooner had I moved in than he introduced himself as my neighbor on the floor below and invited me in for coffee. I saw his tables bending under the piles of papers and towers of books, I noted the darkened atmosphere. We drank our coffee at a quickly cleared corner of the larger table, I stared around me in disbelief, without paying any more attention to what Florian was talking about, which was some vague literary or cultural topic.

From the second day on, he knew how to arrange things so that he intercepted me on the stairs to invite me for coffee, for a sip of wine, or for dinner, until I began to decline his invitations, saying that I had to work, and that was true, I only went out to take my dog for a walk and do the necessary shopping.

Our encounters soon degenerated into positional warfare. At first, Florian frequently came over as it were in passing to ask if he could do anything for me.

I have to make a quick trip out, he would say. Can I get something for you while I'm out? Or may I quickly make us a pot of coffee? Just a quick one, I'm busy too.

Not today, I have to work, I say, I'll gladly come another time. Many thanks.

Not at all, says Florian, he too is terribly busy. He has writing to do. Just has to dart out for a minute to get something. I hear him rummaging around briefly in his room, and then I hear his footsteps, he bounds nimbly down the stairs, humming a tune. I hear the heavy door fall shut and his quick footsteps receding. A little later he returns with a whole group of people, the stairwell shakes from their trampling, I hear their laughter, the booming voice of my housemate, women's laughter, glasses clinking, now and then Florian's rapid steps between his room and his kitchen as he serves his guests, thick clouds of smoke rise up, including the dense smoke of cigars. His invitations and orgies of eating and drinking stretch through the nights and into the morning hours, by noon things seem more civilized again, sometimes behind a closed door, a tête-à-tête? Now and then Florian brings astonishingly pretty young women home with him. For a while, he goes on climbing the stairs to my room to invite me "just for a little drink" with his guests. I forcefully decline.

Damn it, Florian, I say rudely, I've already told you so often, I don't have time, I have to keep to my schedule, it can't be changed. Leave me alone.

From then on, when we meet in the stairwell, Florian exhibits a new type of affected behavior. Now he's abrupt.

Have to work, he says right away with no hackneyed phrases, have to write.

That won't be very easy with all the things piled on your table, and all your socializing, I'd like to know where you intend to do your work—the remark unfortunately slips out of me.

That'll be quite simple, he says. I just have to clean up. It's long overdue.

The next time we meet in the stairwell, he murmurs with no prelude:

I'm in a hurry, I have to clean my room.

I don't answer. But from now on, upstairs at my table, I listen intently for Florian's arrival. He hurries upstairs, taking two steps at a time, and unlocks his door. I listen. Scraping sounds, silence. I see him in my mind's eye, I see him in his coat, his pupils' assignments or books under his arm, standing in his room jammed full with everything, and peering with his little eyes at all the sediment, the room is strewn with crumbs, stained with wine, scattered with cigarette ash, it smells of cheese and the remains of other food, those telltale signs of years of suppression, and he panics. He has to make room. But where to begin? And where was he suddenly supposed to find the strength and endurance, the will, the discipline, the courage, the sheer élan? I know, no: I feel that he notices at this very moment that I'm eavesdropping on him, that I *see* him through all the walls, I'm keeping him under surveillance. One person keeping a watchful eye on the other, deathly silence. Then the door opens, he goes down the stairs, rather hesitantly, he forces himself to take measured steps, just don't run, he says to himself, now he starts to whistle, he's whistling something that at first sounds more like a hiss, a humming through his teeth, he's trying to give the impression of a man who just happens to be going out.

He stays out a long time. Days with and days without Florianian banquets. His absences are irregular, sometimes for days on end.

Oh, you live in that writers' building? people ask me, that's where that . . . what's his name . . . teacher, who's working on a book, right, his name is Florian.

And now I imagine him, with his expansive gestures, making some newly picked-up friends believe that he is of course terribly busy, he's writing a book, yes, he's been working on it for a long time, but just now he has a quarter of an hour's time, so they could quickly, but just a coffee or a small sip, no more, couldn't they . . . Besides, he would like it if they came to visit him from time to time. You can find the building easily, it's a real scriptorium, the building. The man who lives above me is a writer too, you should know, he says. You can't miss it, not even at night, you can recognize the building by the lit upper windows, a real lighthouse.

Our encounters on the stairs are more reserved, Florian narrows his eyes behind his glasses, cautiously keeping his distance, then he forces a pained smile as he squeezes past me. Otherwise, he stays out of my way.

I have a double door installed outside my workroom, I want to put some space between Florian and me, want to shut him out of my life. But as I sit at my gigantic desk, with my back to the windows, my gaze directed at the double door, I catch myself thinking: so he's going around saying he's writing a book, the liar, and he can't even be alone with himself for a second. The weakling, I think, he flees from himself, always has to run after other people who will hold his hand, this massive exploiter, blood-sucker, vampire, rascal, destroyer, smoocher, sponger, repulsive creep, vermin, this bastard, I mutter. And, at that, he is free, has all the freedom in the world, and what does he do with it? And now it occurs to me that at the beginning of our acquaintance he was always going around with one of my books, as people told me, and he pretentiously gave recitations from it, as people informed me, gave recitations and readings with his Rhaeto-Romanic accent, as if we had written the book together. And now I see him in front of me, selling me, yes, as if we were a team, with me being the writer, the one who works it out in detail, while he . . . reads aloud from it; as if I were his clerk; in truth, I think, he must have been downright relieved when I showed up, now he was really free, I was his alibi, the typewriter was clattering day and night, *our* typewriter, while he gave recitations and received ovations, carried on the business, kept the public interested. His jovial laughter, I think, always happy. Would you like some coffee, may I fix you something to eat? how about a glass of wine? He uses up whole armies of people to take away his time and keep him from getting anything done, he always has to go to new districts to seek them out, the people are used up so quickly, they start to see through him. Don't talk such foolish nonsense, I once heard someone say to him.

And I throw myself into my work at my typewriter, cursing with rage, is this life? I want to write myself out of it, just let me finish this book . . . And I thought, I had imagined the life of a writer to be entirely different, not like mine, quickly taking the dog out, darting dirty looks at people as I lurk around street corners, tugging at the leash, have you finally finished sniffing, you beast of a dog? Florian's mother: tall, gaunt, makes an austere impression; he goes to visit her every few weeks. Did I mention that Florian has unusually large hands, very, very large and warm hands that one always notices with surprise when shaking hands with him, or when he's cutting bread or slicing cheese, when he's pouring wine, then one thinks with amazement, what indecently large hands he has, obviously also very strong hands, in any case his hands are always too large for cutting bread or cutting up cheese, and one imagines his hands away from the loaf of bread and imagines how they are likely to behave when they're on the delicate body of a young girl. Another reason his hands are probably so astonishing is because his eyes are so small. And sometimes there's something in his look that tells me that he's very well informed, something knowing, even pleading, that can make one feel ashamed. He has a generally strange appearance, he's impressively tall, strongly built and plump, but the plumpness doesn't really stand out, and he has a relatively small head with black, parted hair. And glasses. And behind the glasses his small eyes are always on their guard and draw even closer together when he feels offended, either by me or someone else. He has the appearance of an escaped monk, or just of an escapee in general. When I see him walking, there's something boyish about him, like a plump, rugged little boy, and it would hardly be surprising if he suddenly started to hop on one leg, because after all, he has just *escaped* from school. There's a trustfulness about him, an expectation that people will be kind. If he sees someone he knows, he greets the person effusively. The slightest gesture that could be interpreted as an invitation causes him to approach, but he does so with a certain guardedness, a readiness to retreat, as seen in someone who has all too often had bad experiences. Someday, with his gigantic hands, he's going to strangle someone, his chatter is just the admission fee, he's been seeking admission for so long that someday he will have had enough.

Good Heavens, I think now in my narrow boxroom: maybe I

was the one who gave him that plan, maybe he had no plan at all before I moved into the building, maybe it's like the fellow with the long beard who always slept well until someone asked him if he put his long beard over or under the cover when he went to bed, and after that he couldn't get to sleep anymore, he didn't know what he did with his beard, he had never asked himself about it, and maybe Florian had never been bothered by his free time at all, maybe I just happened to ask him in passing how he spent his time, and it wasn't until that moment that he began to think of having a plan or of the necessity of having a plan, began to believe in it and to blather on about it, and after that he felt obliged to have a plan.

Is it possible that I, by my presence in the building, placed him under an incommensurable, unbearable, ridiculous pressure to work harder and do well, that I caused him to criticize himself? He became my double, my other self, as it were, he was claiming all the glory for himself—is that what so infuriated me? Did I begrudge the fact that he borrowed my damned writing and clattering at the typewriter to make himself look good? He was only borrowing me for harmless rhetorical purposes, so why not. He slipped, as it were, into one sleeve of my person, nothing more, yet I took it so terribly amiss. O Florian, or did I envy you your never-ending free time and freedom, your lifestyle, of which I felt incapable, for some wretched reason, dependent as I was on the typewriter, the ironing table, bound to the idea that I had to be an achiever?

Florian lived below me, but above me, in an attic room right next to the storage space under the roof, another fellow tenant put in guest appearances, sometimes just for a few hours. He was a teacher too, a Latin teacher, if I'm not mistaken. I was also painfully aware of his arrivals and his presence, I couldn't come to terms with the fact that this gentleman was there.

He had the habit or bad habit of scurrying up the stairs, usually in the late afternoon, but mornings too, and for no other reason than he was so obviously trying to flit past me as considerately and as invisibly as possible, I had to listen and make myself aware of this fellow I didn't like, I found him physically revolting, he had that five o'clock shadow that people with a heavy growth of beard retain even right after they shave, which means they always have it, and his five o'clock shadow made the pasty texture of his face stand out, in which his dark eyes peered out from behind his glasses with an expression that was both slightly ironic and also fearful or reproachful. So he always tried to get past me without making a sound, if possible on tiptoe, and this maneuver, designed to be considerate and quiet, sounded louder to my ears than any possible clatter.

But something else irritated me about the gentleman: he used my bathroom. I had rented the entire floor, and the bathroom belonged to that floor, it was a very narrow room, a tunnel or strip of a room, with a throne right under the small window and a little basin along the wall. Some predecessor had nailed a poster to the inside of the door, and I used to turn my eyes and thoughts toward it while I was sitting there, I no longer know what the poster portrayed, it didn't bother me, but it did bother me and anger me no end that this gentleman had the habit of spending hours in my bathroom, leaving splashes all over the room, I assume he washed himself there, washed himself entirely, didn't just shave or wash his hands but stood there naked and washed himself from top to toe.

The overly long séances in my bathroom made this additional fellow tenant even more disagreeable to me. So I attempted, at first trying to be courteous, to prevent him from using my bathroom to such an extent, indeed from monopolizing it, and asked him not to use it at all, pointing out to him that it belonged to my floor and was even included in my lease under a special clause. He objected that this bathroom had to be regarded as a sort of shared bathroom because there was no toilet upstairs in the attic and he had always used my toilet, since long before I had moved into the building, his right to it was at least as established a right, and that caused me to ask the lady who owned the building about it, whereupon she offered to rent the attic room in question to me, since I had already expressed interest in it and would have had a use for it; for her part, she was quite prepared to throw out the gentleman living in the attic, apparently she too disliked him.

And then one day this Latin teacher came to me, he had, he said, heard that I was trying to drive him out, that was the reason why he had come and the reason for the discussion that he was hereby requesting. He sat on my old sofa that I had once purchased in England, sat there with his legs crossed and his eyes wide open and fearful and said, as he asked my permission to go into some detail, that the fact was that he was attached to this attic room because as a child, a farmer's child, no city child, a child of poor people who had many children, as far as I understood, he had lived in an attic room that was also directly next to a storage space or a dark storage hole, and this attic room of his childhood was what he had found again in this attic room here that he had already occupied for such a long time, in any case for much longer than I had been there, he couldn't imagine another attic room, another room, even if he could find one, which was doubtful, because this room here simply meant more, for him quite personally much more, and it meant more than just an attic room, it embodied the situation of his childhood, a spiritual topos, and besides, he was deaf in one ear and his physician had recently told him he was in danger of losing his hearing altogether, the process was unstoppable, he wanted to make sure I understood that, unstoppable, and it would have dire consequences, because sooner or later it would probably cause him to lose his position as a teacher, and for that reason too the attic room was important to him, absolutely necessary, indeed necessary for his survival, this was where he did his writing, he was writing a novel, I should know, and when it came to the point where he had to give up his position as a teacher, he would have to earn his living from his novel and other things he would write, which he begged me to understand, and writing, that is, continuing to write the novel and to finish it was only possible for him, it was particular to his own personal needs, in an attic room like this one that embodied the attic room of his childhood, because back then the neighboring room had also been a storage space, he needed this incarnation of his childhood room in order to write, that is, in order to survive, and that was why he couldn't possibly think of leaving the attic room, it was unimaginable to him, he would have to be removed by force, but, and he wanted to point this out with all due emphasis, he would have to interpret my overtures as psychological terrorism, and I would probably not want to boast about having used psychological terrorism on a man who was in danger of losing his hearing . . .

So once again we have a writer and a novelist in the building, I thought, but I've never come across anything to read by this gentleman and attic poet, never heard that he'd published anything, he was and remains a Latin teacher, and in his attic room he was often visited by young girls, female pupils came and went, maybe he gave them private lessons, maybe his ablutions were associated with these visits. He stayed put.

I don't know why I'm writing all this, I'm here in Paris, not only hundreds of kilometers but also a lifetime away from that gentleman and far removed from the living conditions of that time, but now the man with the five o'clock shadow is here in this boxroom and I'm getting worked up about him, just as the old dove man sits across from me and puts on his exhibition, there have always been people who annoyed me and angered me. They got too close to me, no, they upset me too much. The doves in our courtyard don't coo, the sound they make is more like a moan, an insistent, indecent moaning. But the turtledove sounds even worse, it makes a sort of truncated cock-a-doodle-doo or cuckoo call, a scream that is shortened and modified to three notes, it cries out a little scale, repeating it in exactly the same way without any variation more than ten, sometimes twenty times at a go, so that I automatically start to count as with the chiming of a clock, it's as if I absolutely have to count, as if it were a matter of great importance. Then the roaring of the old man again, the shrill voice of his wife, is that life? not to mention the joy of freedom. Joy is a yellow banana, someone once wrote to me, I think he wrote me that from South America.

In the building with the two teachers who both pretended to be writers, our Fräulein Murz lived on the second floor in a tiny room, but spent more of her time in the tiny kitchen right next to it. When I say room, that's not correct, she actually lived in the stairwell. She had at one time been the cleaning woman for the lady who owned the building, and now that she was over seventy, she had the right to stay on here, like an old horse put out to pasture.

Fräulein Murz was a hunchback, she walked bent over at a right angle, besides that she had a goiter, and since she was also a very small person, these two deformities made her seem like someone from a fairy tale, she looked like a little witch or like a goblin, in any case not like a modern human being. She sat on one of the creaking, squeaking wooden steps and thumbed through papers, newspapers, and advertising supplements, the latter were thrown down in piles below the mailboxes. Her relationship to newspapers and wastepaper in general was a mania, insofar as it appealed to her desire to collect things, and since she could barely read, she pretended she was reading on the stairs, like a child. In addition, this activity also served another purpose: she placed herself as a living obstacle on the stairs so that she could keep an eye on everything, the stairwell was her sovereign territory, and if a stranger came into the building, then she wanted to know to whom he was paying a visit, she saw herself as a sentinel.

She smelled bad, and her kitchen stank so badly that it made me retch, the kitchen didn't just stink of cooking odors, but also of something that made me think of feces; when she bought her groceries she preferred to buy meat scraps and that sort of thing, although she wasn't poor, we knew that, she was miserly. She also made soups, if you went past her, she might blurt out without a greeting or introductory remark: made potato soup, fine, is good for gout.

She said it apodictically, without directly addressing anyone, so that one was faced with the alternative of either saying nothing, of ignoring the remark and going past her without saying a word, or of taking up the topic, and it made me angry every time. Because when I did condescend to make a remark, it could well happen that she immediately gave me a real earful. She had thick lips, and these lips slobbered too, because she had long since lost her teeth. When she spoke, I always had to stare at that thick growth, then my gaze wandered to her drooping goiter, I couldn't help it, and as I did so, she looked right back at me with a downright lascivious gleam in her little eyes that continually flickered back and forth, alternating between a shy approach, almost servile flirtation, and curt dismissal. Just as she lured you unasked into a conversation by commenting on her dinner, and then, if you replied, acted as if you were being pushy—she also enjoyed speaking about her former beauty or physique. She would say: I had much more beautiful legs than her there, *that one*! pointing at your female companion who is perhaps entering the building for the first time and knows nothing of Fräulein Murz, and as she says it her thick growth of a mouth makes smacking sounds, and to lend emphasis to her statement she points yet again with her crooked fingers at the lady's legs, and the lady stands there dismayed or embarrassed or amused, as the case may be, and then Fräulein Murz turns away and makes her characteristic gesture of dismissal that's supposed to indicate that she has had enough, she lowers her head with its straggly hair tied up at the back and twisted into a tiny bun, then she sighs and gives us to understand that the conversation is over. Or she looks up at me with that expectant stare. But, but, Fräulein Murz, I might say, and if I say it in as deep a bass voice as I can manage, in the voice of a good-natured amateur equestrian, a school principal, or even just a teacher, then it can happen that she gives in to me with her groveling smile. Or if I don't react, because I'm lost in thought about something else, she merely repeats her assertion with greater emphasis. She can also break off the conversation abruptly. There's always something of a power struggle at work with our Fräulein Murz, who claims to be a German, the child of farmers in Baden, and as she once told me, she took a job in Marseille when she was thirteen, that was the beginning of her career, she had Japanese ancestors on her mother's side of the family, she once maintained.

When I had just moved into the building and still knew nothing of its internal relationships, in particular nothing of the balance of power, Fräulein Murz used to come into my room unasked. I'd be sitting at my big table, the ironing table, my back to the windows as always, when the door opened and Fräulein Murz came in with a broom and dustpan in her hands, her head and nose directed at the floor, she literally came rolling in, without knocking or even saying hello, then she was inside and started approaching my table, dusting and knocking things about. She's not right in the head, I thought, and told her emphatically to leave. No, no, she crowed, she *had* to do it, she had to do the cleaning throughout the building, she squawked and carped and stubbornly fended off all objections. I said, *let's get this straight once and for all*, I said, I did not wish to have my room cleaned and would not tolerate it, she should get it through her head once and for all, I said, and from then on she only came now and then, as if for a visit, or she approached me in such a way as to test my response, announcing her presence from afar, banging her broom against the wooden stairs as she approached from below, that was her way of doing things, her broom and dustpan were the insignia of her power, but also her magic wands, with which she gained access everywhere. She often stayed a while outside my double door, stayed there banging and dusting outside the threshold of my room. If I opened the door, then she came in, if I didn't move, she withdrew again.

She loved rubbish, all kinds of rubbish, her room, people said, was not furnished with a bed and that sort of thing, but filled up with nothing but crumpled paper, it was a real mouse-hole where Fräulein Murz slept or spent the night. This room was always carefully locked because its contents were valuable to her and were her very own, but also because she kept money hidden under the rags and newspapers, people said she hoarded small change and silver coins in big paper bags. When she left the room to go out and do her shopping or errands, she first locked her door with a big key, then she walked a few steps away from the door, then she turned around very fast, snuck back to the door, and began shaking the latch as if to make sure that it and the lock had not deceived her while she'd had her back turned. Deceived, betrayed, I don't know what she expected, but she anticipated all kinds of pranks and nasty tricks on the part of the door. She went away and snuck back, rattled at it to catch the evil door or latch red-handed. When she went out, which she announced to everyone long in advance, she wore a black coat that reached down to the ground, it went over the hump of her back and down to the ground, and at the front it likewise fell loosely down over her feet, she must have been given this coat by some gracious lady, and now, when she went out, she had also combed her unwashed hair, which was twisted into that little bun. In addition to wearing the black coat, she also took the cane, a fine cane equipped with a silver handle—or was it an umbrella?—supported by this cane or umbrella, she went along, casting her lecherous little eyes to the left and right, standing still every few steps, turning and looking in all directions, until she chose her course, and if there happened to be a couple standing down by the water, the building was located close to a river, stairs led down to it, stairs that Florian, for example, used to take, hopping and full of wonder; so if two lovers were standing there, which was not uncommon, and the two of them were embracing, or had thrown their arms around each other's necks, if they were kissing each other just then, Fräulein Murz liked to position herself beside them to address the two of them unexpectedly, but not with a question, a greeting, or that sort of thing, no, she would say abruptly, presumably giving the people thus torn out of their kiss the fright of their lives: made potato soup today, fine, is good for gout, and so on

She went out to go shopping, but more to accost people, these crazies always have an exhibitionist streak, I find, just as I have the impression that the dove man comes out from behind his window more frequently and more loudly than usual to hit at the doves when I happen to have company over.

Fräulein Murz said, as I was walking past her, something like: The Hungarianers have shot three dogs onto the sun again. Now, as an answer, I can either say: But, but Fräulein Murz, the *Hungarians* have nothing to shoot, you mean the Russians, or do you mean the Americans? But even they don't shoot at the sun, and why three dogs at once, what makes you think that; but hardly have I thought of saying all that than I see the ridiculousness of it, there *is* no answer to such a remark. But if I were to give her a jovial answer to that effect, then she would insist on it: it's what I've heard, it's true, this and that person said it. If I say nothing, then she makes this dismissive gesture. Her favorite topic is murder. Someone's done someone else in, she says, *did him in*, she loves the expression, I *did in* the rat, she maintained—

One time, it was on a Sunday, I was pounding at the typewriter with the door open, because on this day not even the Latin teacher had put in an appearance, when I heard Fräulein Murz rummaging around and singing in the stairwell, I forgot to mention that she liked to sing when she was in a good mood, and had a frail, breaking voice that sometimes seemed to hang by a very thin thread. Her favorite songs were children's songs like "Alle Vögel sind schon da," *All the birds are here already*, or "O du fröhliche o du selige . . ." *O you merry, O you blessed*, she sang that Christmas carol even in summer, and she sang "Stille Nacht, heilige Nacht" *Silent night, holy night* in all seasons, but now she was singing "O geh nicht fort o bleib bei mir, mein Herz ist ja dein Heimatort" *Don't go away, o stay with me, my heart is your true home.* I heard it, forgot about it, heard it getting louder, closer and closer, and then, I opened my eyes wide, she appeared in the doorway, she literally crept across my field of vision toward me, and she was half naked, under her hanging goiter were two old woman's breasts, and she was holding her likewise naked, withered arms over her breasts as if she were doing gymnastics exercises and was swinging them to the side, she entered my room with a grin. I was paralyzed with horror, but then I called out, I forced myself to say: but, but Fräulein Murz, practicing nudism, are you, you'll catch your death of cold, quickly, get some clothes on, go away, but make it fast, you don't want to get sick. I screamed all sorts of such sayings at her from behind my table, behind my barricade.

Is it just that I'm incapable of keeping the proper distance from people? Do I let everyone get too close, take them too personally? That's how it is with the Arabs here in this part of town, first you feel sorry for them, no, first I found it exotic to live in a quarter populated to a great degree, if not predominantly, by immigrants, or the children of immigrants, Arabs, Africans; the latter standing at street corners as if on watch, as if standing on one leg and keeping a lookout, as if with a spear at their sides, no, I was ashamed of the image as it came to me, but there it was, I stood revealed as the parochial Züricher I thought I'd escaped, seeing the beautiful Parisian street with its system of sewers transforming itself into an endless steppe. How many such thoughts, prejudices, racist clichés of that sort were present in me without my being aware, poisoning my mind? In this quarter, the Africans and Arabs stand around, it seems, all day long; unemployed and without proper accommodations, I know, they'll be living in some dump of a room in one of the most dilapidated residential hotels, that's why they stand on the street, or down below in their bars, what else is there for them to do. Say I've lined up for a wicket at the post office, and a black man is standing in front of me or beside me, probably fantastically dressed, the colors, the combination of colors, utterly individual in style, against his dark or black skin the colors naturally look entirely different than against white skin, white skin soon looks dirty and worn-out and becomes utterly submerged in too much color; there are also people who go around in their national costume, with these wide, often white coats or coat-shaped capes, with or without a hood, that reach down to the ground, magnificent gowns that make me think of the King from the East, the fellows who wear that sort of thing are usually gigantic, they must be two meters tall; so let's say I'm standing waiting in line, and then I'm startled because I find I'm the only Caucasian in the building, and I feel both threatened and somehow inconsequential, I take everyone and everything as a personal critique, and that man over there is filling out a piece of paper, a form, but with a golden or gold-plated fountain pen that looks particularly precious in his dark hand, which is light, though, and pale on the inside; is that what I'm here to do too? Why is that somehow surprising to me, that we do the same things, that we have the same errands to run, and now I wonder was I really so far gone as all that, had I really led such a sheltered life to that point? Their presence alone was exciting, their appearances so excitingly different, they astonished me over and again, their voices so much more physical, so to speak, or physical in a different way, than the voices I was used to hearing, their voices gutturally good-natured with an inherent roll or an inherent rumble of thunder to them—sexy, as people say. And then, they love to laugh, they laugh about nothing at all and slap their thighs, bent over with laughter. Their laughter often rolls and thunders for hours in my courtyard; once or twice recently a family gave a party that lasted until three in the morning or later, always the leading voice and then the laugh chorus, good-natured and infectious; what are they laughing about like that, I wondered, and, another impertinence, I began to say to myself that they had nothing to laugh about, really, so how, in spite of it all, can they still be enjoying themselves so much?

And sometimes, for example when I'm dozing in the Metro and

then suddenly become aware of and take in the man or woman across from me, become aware of them thanks to the forced, indecent proximity of sitting across from one another, and maybe our knees are touching . . . I lose myself in the dark, foreign face, I feed on the dark skin that may be really jet-black or ebony and glistening as with dew, the splendidly sparkling irises swimming in the alabaster setting of the whites of their eyes, their mouths with the shimmering pink inner flesh of their lips; I stare in wonder at the extremely bold peaked or Mao caps, the hats, the derbies, or simply the hair that's been twisted into those little antennae or decorated with a thousand little buns; their fantastic clothing, their disguises—but wait, where did I come up with the idea of their being in disguise? there are, incidentally, jackets of a particular cut that you never see on white people, these jackets are like tailcoats that reach down to the knees, tightly fitted at the waist, they have such high shoulders that they look like incipient wings. They strike me as sort of friendly, gentle. Of course, there are also the militant, confrontational kind of black men who get onto the train in riveted leather, in boots with pointed, steel-reinforced toes, open aggression on their faces. And the street sweepers, leaning on their brooms.

They're not like us, maintains the concierge, and they always come with so many children. Once, actually even a short time ago, the street was entirely white, he says, whereas now it's getting increasingly dark. Soon, on Place Vendôme, instead of Rolls-Royces and Maseratis parked outside the Ritz, we'll see kneeling camels chewing their cud, he says, and I tense up at this echo of my own ugliness. Soon there'll be a camel market there, if things keep on like this, says the concierge, and I find myself thinking two things at once, *suits me fine* and *what a shame.*

By contrast, the Arabs are taciturn and gloomy, careworn, tired. The difference is evident in their bistros and bars, the quarter is full of them; if someone asks me where I live in Paris, I answer that I live in the couscous quarter, this staple of the Arab diet is as indigenous here as *choucroute* in Alsace.

The Arab bistros are plain and somehow the color of sand, it seems to me as if even the air is sandy, a desert atmosphere, clichés are a disease, and the people who stand there at the bar, often for hours on end, without consuming anything, who linger in these subterranean rooms, have this mixture of false subservience, mistrust, and hatred in their faces, the expression of a poor relation. And they are always just bars for men, in contrast to the African bars, where men turn up with their wives and sisters and mistresses and children and entire families, and they laugh and palaver and the narrow room is charged with their physical charisma, one is seized by their physicality or sex as if by a whirlpool, even their voices.

The Arabs aren't only a minority, if a very large minority, they're the poor relations of the nation, they're foreign workers, and it seems to me they aren't welcome here. Most of them are here without their wives or families, so they're more than doubly alone. When I was first in Paris, I liked to frequent a bar called Said's, Said himself maintained he was a Kabyle or a Berber and not "merely" an Algerian, thereby wanting to give himself a higher racial rank, so to speak, although, stocky and chubby as he was, at least in outward appearance he did not seem to belong to this elite at all. I liked it at Said's because the cylindrical iron stove gave off a pleasant warmth, but perhaps I was there because I too felt the need to keep a low profile, I certainly didn't want anything to do with any cultural cliques, and I didn't want to associate with the artists and intellectuals in the Latin Quarter or in Saint-Germain, that was the last thing I wanted. It's likely that I also had this dark, proud sense of shame, I don't really know where it came from, but I too felt like a sort of pariah, I sat in my boxroom and was ashamed of my blockade, of my unused freedom and free time, of my longing for protection and direction, of my fear, and so I quickly went across the street to Said, who always received me with this embarrassed laughter, he was embarrassed because he thought I was "better," I was usually the only non-Arab, and he was also embarrassed by his brothers. I took cover at Said's, and I also liked his cooking, done in an unspeakable hole of a back room, this cooking was, God knows, monotonous, either couscous (*mouton, boeuf merguez*) or lamb chops with potatoes, once he also had pasta, I liked it all. Said called out the order to someone he called CHEF in the back room, where someone really was doing the cooking, it was a tired old man. I appreciated the considerate treatment, the friendliness, the respect, as time went on, I actually had rights at Said's, I was his best customer. And so I sometimes went over in the mornings for a glass of wine or beer, and in the afternoons just to read, and in doing so I was basically not much different from my poor flighty Florian, I fled from the captivity of my boxroom, where I expected myself to get some work done, something significant if possible, and yet I only felt fear, *and there was a gaping hole in my soul like the fly of my pants*, as someone wrote. Said looked at me with a mixture of amusement and genuine joy. As time went on, I could go there even after Said had closed for the day, he had nothing to do other than run his business, he slept in a partitioned area above the bistro, and he always wanted to have his family come soon, they'll be here next month, he was always saying, my family will follow me here. But they never came, maybe he didn't have a family at all. And one day, after I'd been away for a week, when I came back I wanted to go right over to Said's as usual, which was my way of going undercover again, but instead of Said, a tall, sinister, squint-eyed man was standing behind the bar. He was Said's successor, during my absence Said had sold the bistro or the *affaire*, as they call it here, I never saw him again, and that was the end of my shelter.

Why am I actually here? I asked myself, it's not as if I've taken an oath. I felt that way when I hadn't seen another person for a long time, when I hadn't spoken with anyone, when I thought I couldn't bear being alone any longer; when I started being so ashamed of my loneliness that I snuck through the streets: I was ashamed that I felt inconsolable, and I feared people could see my state of mind on my face. If only I lived in a cheerful, entertaining quarter, I thought, and not in this *quartier couscous* that was getting increasingly darker and even more weighed down with the problems of our new arrivals.

It's my aunt's apartment, it's her apartment that she left to me, that's *one* reason for my being here.

I was familiar with several of my Parisian aunt's apartments, incidentally, my mother had also had a Parisian aunt whom she visited now and then, back when we were kids and my mother was still a young woman. Back then, it was still considered chic when one suddenly had to go to Paris because of relatives, and when my mother returned from such trips, in my eyes she looked like an elegant foreigner, like a young lady from Paris.

I was familiar with several of my aunt's apartments, but this one here was the worst of them. She had owned this apartment for a long time, but had rented it out; she herself lived in a somewhat better apartment in the vicinity of Daumesnil, in a *quartier résidentiel*, as she liked to maintain, with some exaggeration. Shortly before her death she had sold the better apartment, to a musician and composer, and with the proceeds from that she had moved into this tiny dwelling to spend her twilight years here as a pensioner, she was already over seventy, and Montmartre, by the way, which is on the border between the eighteenth and the ninth arrondissements, had always been her quarter, so she was actually just returning home.

When I headed toward Rue Simart on that summer morning in 1973, in search of my aunt's new home, I was very curious, but soon disappointed. This street is admittedly like thousands of other Parisian streets, and yet it seemed a bit gloomier to me, the stone here is a bit grimmer than usual—or dirtier? and has nothing at all in common with that white and ocherous gray that makes such an expensive impression, those cubist colors on façades that look like coated paper flaking off. They suck up and spit back the beams cast by the city of light in so incomparable a manner that one can't help but call it spiritual. Here, though, the gray seemed brownish or dirty gray, in short, it seemed to me as if I was marching straight into a tunnel. Here, too, as in the rest of the city, one store or little shop stood next to another, but these shops were without awnings, a bicycle dealer, a wallpaper salesman, a grocer, a tool supplier, an employment agency, a pinball machine refinisher, a restorer of old furniture, a fur-coat mender, a health-food store, a real-estate agency, shops so introverted it was as if their owners lived in caves and didn't conduct their business along the sidewalks as is done almost everywhere else in Paris, they might just as well have had their stores in the catacombs. Even the sky was barely visible here, as if it were something that only happened elsewhere.

In the semi-darkness of the corridor in the building, a woman called out after me, and when I asked her where my aunt lived, she directed me to the back, which faced the courtyard, to the third floor, the door on the right. I knocked, and after waiting for some time I pressed the old-fashioned doorbell that gave off a buzzing sound, after which I first heard the growling and barking of a dog and then my aunt's mistrustful voice. Without opening the door, she asked from the inside if I was the mailman. I answered: It's me, your nephew, your nephew from Switzerland, yes, it's me, in the flesh, flesh and blood, please open the door, *ma tante*, I said, addressing her as "ma tante" in the same tone as one might say "mon general." And the door opened at last, and she appeared, and she was still in her bathrobe, not yet dressed or made-up for the day, but she was unmistakably herself, even if somewhat thinner than I had remembered. She was very short, my aunt, she carried a considerable bulge, a bust like the bow of a ship, on her skinny legs, and had a quite large, pert nose, and in contrast to these bulges or up-turned features, she had small eyes, and her face was usually perfectly made-up under hair that she kept dyed blonde to the last. Her hands seemed to think for themselves, because her head was always somewhere else. She liked to hold her head slightly inclined to the side, which made her seem thoughtful, even absentminded. While her independent hands cooked and set the table and distributed all sorts of odds and ends, such as serviettes, a wine carafe, bread, and salt and pepper shakers on the table and the side-table, she went around with such a thoughtful look. What's she thinking about, I wondered, is she thinking of the past, is she going over sad memories? The apartment looked different back then, it was jam-packed with rather cheaply ostentatious furniture, and the television seemed monumental on its stand. While "ma tante" ran around with dainty movements and tiny steps between the furniture that was blocking everything, her fox terrier Jimmy pattered around with even tinier, but exceptionally fast, scratching steps. He had gotten rotund and unkempt. My aunt always had dogs, and they were always called Jimmy or Tobe. The last one, Jimmy, I don't know how many Jimmys she'd had by then, was a strange dog, he ate only when there were witnesses, and toward the end of his life he ate only when one pretended that one was going to go out, right away. My aunt put on her coat and made other preparatory gestures, or she lifted the telephone receiver and told an imaginary friend the important news that they would be going out right away, and this made Jimmy race for his food. They were always nagging at each other, just like an old married couple, nothing that Jimmy did was unworthy of comment to my aunt, either she smothered him with affection or she yelled at him and cursed him utterly. She alternated between the two tones without transition, which is why this Jimmy, like all his predecessors, by the way, was not only cranky, but also slightly crazy.

I last saw my aunt laid out in the hospital mortuary in Evian, where she had spent her holidays, and after feeling slightly unwell, she had been sent by the physician to the hospital, where she promptly died. She lay like a strange army commander in dry ice, she lay like that for a long time because the hospital wasn't equipped with a freezer, and also because she couldn't be buried without the necessary papers, and in order to procure these papers and to take care of everything else as well, the police had notified me and summoned me to Evian, obviously my aunt carried my address with her at all times for the event of an emergency. So I saw her for the last time in the Evian hospital, Jimmy had remained at the hotel, I had the porter hand him over to me, and the police gave me the keys and my aunt's few things, her suitcases, and I traveled with all of it to Paris. I now entered my aunt's apartment with power of attorney, I had to sift through all her papers and then complete the formalities, I had to liquidate this aunt's life and whatever was left over from it, it took me weeks, and then I had the apartment to myself, I cleared it out and furnished it to my liking.

The street that had seemed depressing to me on my first visit continues to make the same impression. It's dreary, leads nowhere, only to itself, and this self is as shabby as an unshaven face, somehow dirty, the impression of dirtiness somehow associated with poverty or dilapidation, it's a street people have given up on, written off, Rue Simart, the name belongs to an architect, I read, Monsieur Simart was a very enterprising gentleman, very busy, just as Eugène Sue was a popular author, the two of them, I mean the two streets, intersect at the corner, but aside from that there is truly not a grain of culture or art in the air here.

I've been asking myself for some time what it is about the call of the turtledove that forces me to listen to it and count the number of cries, it sounds like the endlessly repeated call of the cuckoo in a cuckoo clock. It's a call like panpipes getting started, a three-note sob, a cry of misery, if nothing else, and since it sounds at all hours of the day or night, it's often unbearable. By the way, it's the only noise here that really bothers me. Below me is a lodger who gives guitar lessons and plays organ concertos so loudly that they make my apartment vibrate, but he is significantly less of a nuisance than that hopeless call for help from the turtledove.

I want out into the world, I want to live outside in the world, I don't want to be in Zürich anymore, I thought back then, not on those few streets and squares that are always the same, where I take my dog for a walk and everyone knows who I am, my thoughts went along those or similar lines, and then I said to myself *Now or Never*, when I got offered this apartment, this stroke of luck that my own aunt had given me with her demise, I sensed a new beginning, it was presumptuous of me at the time to *hope* for a new beginning, and then I departed.

I took a berth on the train from Zürich and fell asleep almost immediately. I woke up in Basel, I had heard my name being called loudly, yes, I didn't doubt for a moment that the loudspeaker, with those cracking distortions and detonations that are characteristic of all loudspeaker voices in train stations, had called out my name. I sat up with a start, rolled the window down, and looked out anxiously in all directions, always expecting that someone in uniform would appear, confirming my fear, my trepidation. But what was I afraid of? I was traveling legally, I had handed over my passport and ticket to the sleeping-car conductor in accordance with the regulations, and still I was afraid, was I afraid of this exodus? because I was leaving Switzerland and traveling into the *world*, I want to go out into the world, those words had been sounding so long inside of me, as if Zürich was not a part of the world. During the long switching of cars between the Swiss and the French train stations, this being pushed across the border and back again, this indecisive back and forth, I kept a lookout for my pursuers, but then we rode on, and I didn't fall asleep for a long time, now I was afraid the train would derail, I felt the wheels clattering and jolting on the rails, and the train raced and raced along, I thought the engineer must have gone crazy, the train was doing at least two hundred kilometers an hour, and on my bed I felt the rails just managing to hold the racing wheels, but for how long could they continue to do so? And in this state of panic I finally fell asleep, and in my sleep I dreamed I was on a train and the train was racing along, but now in my dream it couldn't go fast enough for me, I began to support its racing with my body, just as one tries to get an open handcart going by rocking one's upper body back and forth, I began to spur on the racing train, I abandoned myself to the ride, and when that wasn't enough, I let the window down and leaned far out, throwing my arms into the air, I was already hanging half outside in this air canal created by the racing train, and then suddenly, on a little square we were just riding past, the main square of a small town, with town hall, church, stately houses, and monument, I saw a girl standing all alone and forsaken there in the deserted square at night, alone with a St. Bernard dog, and as I looked back at the lonely, freezing girl, the orphan, her eyes began to shine, and then a real shower of stars rained out of the child's eyes, a girl with eyes spraying showers of stars? I'd never seen anything like that and didn't know it was possible, I thought in my dream, and then the sleeping-car conductor woke me up to give back my passport and ticket. We were already entering Paris. The train compartment was full of happy mountain climbers, all wearing the same red plaid shirt and the same velvet corduroy climbing pants and the same woolen socks, I stared in wonder at these mountain climbers, and then the voice, the announcer's voice, came to mind, and I was quite relieved to realize that I had slipped through and arrived. Those weren't policemen's voices, pursuers, no, it was my, I mean, it was LA VOCATION. I was in Paris.

Accept me, create me! I cried as I ran around, I won't leave you, I want to be out in the world! I crawled through the thousands upon thousands of prone people's limbs, I strolled, stalked, marched, ran through the streets, with my legs through the lower streets, with my eyes through the upper streets between the rooftops; in the rows of streets with the magnificently channeled sky, the brightest sky in the world, I stood as if in endlessly extended church naves, I saw the sides waft away in the all-enchanting light, they led out and away, the whitish rows of houses, blinking with all the gaps in their Venetian blinds, and I ran along the sidewalks under the awnings on the stores and the bars, beauty before my eyes, I saw it all, I was in it—and yet

I remained outside, a stranger.

And then I took myself off to my boxroom, my home, to this surplus of free time, *He sat there, surrounded by time, and still couldn't capture it*, I once wrote, and that was still the case.

Sometimes one or another of my acquaintances remembered, when he came to Paris, that I lived here now. And since I still didn't have a telephone, it had resulted in several surprising visits, unannounced visits from acquaintances I hadn't seen in a long time. Suddenly they were sitting in my room that looked out on the courtyard, sitting there with faces that reflected their great desire for Paris, a readiness for adventure that they had brought along from Switzerland, they were now really free and *game for anything*, as my Uncle Alois said of himself when he was in a good mood, which didn't really seem to suit him, honest and decent man that he was. But my visitors often had this expectation, so I took them out to show them around the district. We also went through the Arab streets up ahead at Barbès-Rochechouart, through this Orient, and I drew their attention to the lines, the groups of men outside the brothels, there really still were brothels here, if one looked through the barred window in the door one could see half-naked whores of every color and race in the dark corridor inside, heavily made-up faces, flesh bulging out of underwear, like images from Fellini films. The unemployed men without wives or girlfriends stood in lines outside these peepholes, at first I thought they were standing in a line because they had to line up, that the demand was greater than the supply, but of those standing outside, few went in, and seldom at that, most of them were just standing there and picturing to themselves how it would be if they could afford it. We had a sip of white wine or a Ricard at a corner bar, and as we chatted, stimulated both by these exotic activities as well as by seeing each other again, I thought to myself, if only I had stayed home.

My door has three locks, two Yale locks and then a normal European door lock in the middle, as well as a chain across the inside.

My aunt had the locks installed, I see her clearly in my mind's eye, searching for the different keys on her key ring so she can lock the door, she has her little crocodile purse in her other hand, along with the dog leash, and this locking up was always a procedure I found touching as I watched and waited a few steps down. And now, whenever I'm fiddling with all the keys, I see my aunt and myself simultaneously, it's as if the one person is superimposed over the other, and then it seems to me that my fiddling with the keys is not allowed, it's as if I've robbed my aunt, deceived her, done her out of her apartment, if not done her in. She certainly hadn't intended to die when she went to Evian for a holiday, and she probably intended even less to leave me the apartment with everything she owned and all her personal things in it, she hadn't thought of a line of succession, hadn't made a will, she was extremely suspicious, kept everything under lock and key, had three locks to lock herself and everything she possessed inside and to keep intruders out. And now I had acquired it all.

To a certain—sentimental—extent, my aunt was generous, but not open-handed, she was thrifty, economical, mistrustful. She also lived on her own and was entirely reliant on herself, that had always been the case, and that's why she had learned to assert herself, *elle sait se défendre*, as they say here, and part of such behavior is never, under any circumstances, to show one's hand. When I had finished university, she let me know that she wanted to give me a present on the occasion of this great event, my dear boy, she wrote, your aunt doesn't exactly have what might be called a fortune, but she has a sense of commitment to the family, and for having obtained your degree at last, even if it was by dumb luck, she now wanted to give me the money to buy, or pay the first installment on, or finance in some manner, a small used car. During one of my visits to Paris she referred again to her promise, she would, she said with a sigh, give me a thousand Swiss francs on my departure. I was moved and pleased, and during dinner, which we always ate very late, so I didn't have much time left if I wanted to catch the night train, I kept wondering if she had forgotten about it, she made no move to give me the cash. I drank coffee, and after coffee I had one more last glass of wine, then I packed my things, and she still hadn't uttered a word about the money. I won't remind her of it, I thought, either she'll come back to the topic herself, or we'll forget about the whole thing. Then, at the last moment, I was already in my coat, she came up to me with an envelope and a scowl: here, she said, what I promised you, take it, but you'll lose it, won't you?

I said: what can you be thinking, *ma tante*, there's no way I'm going to lose it, I can take care of myself quite well, really, and I thank you very kindly, I appreciate this gift, and believe me, the two of us will both benefit from my having a car. But my aunt just stood there, the envelope in her hand, and then she said: put it in your pocket, my little one, put it in your inside breast pocket, and she unbuttoned my coat and my jacket to see if I had a suitable inside breast pocket. By then I was in a hurry, I put the envelope in my inner breast pocket and, with my aunt's thoughtful eyes on me, started to button up my jacket and coat. Suddenly she said: no, not like that, someone will take the money from you, I know just how it will happen, either they'll steal it from you by jostling you in a crowd, pickpockets have a nose for that sort of thing, or they'll take it away from you when you're sleeping, no, give it to me, she said. And she herself took my coat and jacket off, went with the jacket into the adjoining room, her bedroom, and as I rather impatiently looked to see what was going on, I saw her fumbling with needle and thread, she was sewing shut the breast pocket that contained the envelope.

So, my little one, she said, now we have a solution that should work, *voilà*.

She was satisfied and smiled her slightly sad, melancholic smile, and I kissed her on the cheeks both in thanks and in farewell, no, she said, I'm going with you to the train station, I won't be at peace until I have you in the train car and see the train pull out of the station. Let's go.

No, my aunt would not have given me the apartment, she would not have approved of the way I've taken possession of everything. I see my aunt before my mind's eye when I find myself fiddling with the locks, and now I also see the short, hunchbacked Fräulein Murz, standing like a skier about to descend a slope, in her coat that reaches down to her feet, I see her shaking the latch, turning away, pretending that she's leaving, but then unexpectedly turning back to attack the door and the latch yet again.

NOW I'M AS LIGHT AS A DOVE'S FEATHER, I sometimes said to myself in my boxroom during that initial period in Paris; and as sharp as a stiletto, I added. The lightness came from the fact that I didn't belong to anyone, I was a nonentity; I could wind up in the gutter, I had no past here, did I have a future? I was simply *ready*.

The sharpness was something I hoped to become, I hoped to get it from the city: that it would sharpen me, and sharpen me as it saw fit, just as it liked, whether to live or to die was all the same to me, I wanted it to sharpen me into shape like a pebble. I would put the pebble that I was on my tongue and start to talk. I would speak from a silence light as a stone.

When I talked to myself that way, and I had in fact become accustomed to talking to myself, which is unavoidable, when you're really alone; when I talked to myself that way, I seemed to myself like something numb, so probably something hardy, and hopefully real. And it didn't happen because of self-pity, but on the contrary, out of pride: as if I would soon attain something I had always longed for: to be a feather, the lightest flying object of all, susceptible to the gentlest breath of wind. But the quill, the feather's quill had to be as sharp as a stiletto.

I felt the bones in my head, I pinched my arm, I stared across at the old dove man, I squinted at the piece of sky visible from the courtyard, I said to myself, here I am, here is my boxroom, here is my place. Here is where I'll stay. All that remained of me was myself, whatever that might mean. I was happy, wretchedly happy, so entirely alone in Paris. And I was *free*. Free, too, to go to such establishments as the one run by Madame Julie, and now I ask myself how I even got such an address. I think I got the address from Brisa, a Brazilian woman I met in a bar a long time ago who remained true to me in her own way.

Brisa was a call girl forever changing headquarters and bases of operation, and one of her places was Paris. She called me up here one day, calling her customers was, as I later learned, one of her business practices. She had regular customers in different cities and on different continents, and she kept their phone numbers in a tiny address book she always carried with her, and when she arrived in Paris or New York or Zürich or Rio, she called several numbers one after another, I don't know how she selected them, to announce that she was there and available, should the occasion arise. She didn't go on the street, or in clubs or bars, at least not to work, she worked on a strictly private and discreet basis, always at her own residence. In Paris, she had a small apartment in the 15th arrondissement, on a street that bore the name of a general, I've been in this apartment too, indeed on a day when Brisa wasn't alone, but in the company of a very dark-skinned, taciturn, even off-putting girlfriend whose name I don't remember; she seemed to have just arrived on a surprise visit. We had gone out to dinner together and then the three of us went back to Brisa's apartment. Her apartment was on the seventh floor and consisted of one rather large room with a kitchen, plus a bathtub and a toilet, Brisa had me lie down on the big bed, insisted on taking off my shoes for me, stuffed cushions behind my back, as if I were the beloved, exhausted husband, I lay there and contentedly watched the late show on TV, a large glass of whiskey in my hand, while the two girls whispered next door in the bathroom. Later, I lay on the bed between the two of them, I had stayed mainly from lethargy, from a lethargic need to prolong my contentment. Brisa asked in a whisper if I would like to, which I answered in the affirmative, I would like to, I said, even though I was aware that her very dark-skinned girl-friend was not sleeping, just lying awake, so Brisa ducked under the quilt to judge the size of my erection, the indicator of my readiness, we slipped into each other, and at the same time I could feel this other body on my right, I felt no embarrassment at all, I was as safe and secure as a child in bed with his cousins during the holidays, I was filled with a wonderful feeling of innocence and an effusive love of humanity as the three of us lay there in our different bodies and different skin colors, in this unfamiliar room on the seventh floor of a street that bore the name of a glorious general, it was just as if we were sharing a loaf of bread, as if people thrown together by chance under the canopy of a covered wagon had found a language in which they could communicate, I lay as a guest on another continent, and the sentence was going around in my head WE WERE FLOWING UPSTREAM AND HAD NOTHING TO EAT, I hadn't read that sentence anywhere, it was there, and I didn't know what it meant, but I liked it.

For me, Brisa wasn't a mistress, more like a friend, and one day she started going on about how we should live together. At first I took this suggestion as a mischievous joke, but with time I saw that she meant it seriously, if in a complicated sort of way. I said: how do you picture that working, and why me of all people? I'm anything but solvent, I'm more of a ne'er-do-well, I guess, Brisa, there's no room for two under my roof. I countered with this and similar answers, but Brisa said I had misunderstood her proposal, she would by no means be a burden to me, she would continue working as she had until now, and in Rio she owned a small house, and besides, she wouldn't require me to be faithful, on the contrary, she would introduce me to her girlfriends.

But how do you picture that working? I asked, what would I do in Rio and in your house, which I'm sure is certainly beautiful, would I perhaps sit at the cash register?

You're disgusting, she said. You're pretending to be stupid. Don't pretend to be stupider than you are. But why me of all people? I asked. Why the hell have you got your eye on me?

You, she said, are intelligent and nice, and I can laugh with you. And you'll also be able to do the other thing until you drop dead. So why not you?

Brisa came back to the topic again and again, when she visited me, or when she phoned, and sometimes she phoned in the middle of the night from somewhere very far away, once from America, and the first thing she asked me was always if I was still alone, that is, if

I was living without a girlfriend or a wife. And when I answered in the affirmative, I'm alone, she said I would have to move to Rio to live with her, she would lend me the money for the trip. It was from Brisa that I got the addresses of the *maisons de rendez-vous*, through Brisa that I found my way to Madame Julie. Once, when she had unexpectedly turned up again, but just for a very short time, she said, *meu amor*, she said, I don't like the thought of you sleeping around with any old cow, women are bad, be careful, they'll either fleece you or they'll throw themselves at you. She took out her tiny address book and wrote down one or two addresses from it. There, she said, you have addresses that you won't regret. Say that I sent you, they're admittedly a little more expensive than usual, but you'll be in good hands this way and out of every kind of danger.

Going to a Room; I've often been in such rooms, after I've been there I no longer know how I got there, don't know where the room is located in the building or what street it's on, it remains a room on an unfamiliar continent, but I remember the bed, perhaps the little basin, the scrap of a curtain that billowed in the wind, I remember the sound that I heard at the very moment I entered the room, I'm just passing through, renting the room for an hour, and the sound might have been a child's laugh or a chirp, yes, once it was a chirp, I remember, and for some reason it made me hesitate, a chirp at this hour? I thought, not possible—and went to the window, there, far below on the deserted street, I saw an old woman with a handcart, it was the ungreased, squeaking wheels that made this chirping sound and had made me think for a moment that I heard birds chirping, it was a room to which chirping wheels belonged, and the wheels belonged to a handcart that just happened to be pulled across the godforsaken street at that hour by an old woman. A room, and I'm in this room, as is the woman I've brought here, who is perhaps just then stroking her hair out of her face or tossing it back over her shoulder, so that it looks like a wave of hair, or I think: Hair like a wave, wave of hair; or she says, come and sit down, sit next to me, she says and gestures toward the bed, gestures at the place beside her on the bed, and I'm standing in this room that is small, actually much too small for two people who don't know each other, I light a cigarette, or I take my coat off, and maybe I do sit down on this bed that gives a little beneath me, I feel the hardness or the softness of the mattress as I let myself down on it.

What's your name, I might say, and tell her my name, and she might say, you're not from here or are you passing through, she says something like that and I listen to the sound of her voice, I listen to whether her voice says something or betrays something or communicates something to me, I tune in to my inner self, I listen to the timbre of her voice, which arouses something in me, something I enjoy, a memory, an idea. And later, when Ada takes off her clothes, when we take off our clothes, take off these disguises and cast them aside, I drink in the sight of her thighs, her thighs curving out of her buttocks seem colossal to me, even in such a young person, I adore this sight, it can take my breath away, I don't know why, and her breasts—but that's going much too fast, I can't reconcile the now-distant sight of this beautifully dressed stranger, this stranger who was made up, made to billow out, was girdled in, wearing a skirt and high heels, with the image of this naked woman, that's going too fast, already the distant sight is lost, forgotten, already we're standing flat on our bare feet in this room, where we go to the little basin to wash ourselves, and the way hair falls over the naked back or over the round shoulders of a naked woman looks entirely different from the way hair nestles over a coat or a fur collar, now we are naked, we sit down, lie down on this bed in the room, we touch each other, now I know her voice, know this hint of huskiness or the rolling throatiness that belongs to this voice, and her thighs grow colossal under my groping fingers, it's like your tongue when you have a fever, it's a swelling up that becomes overpowering, the room and my ability to take it in are much too limited for the swelling of her limbs, her thighs, her buttocks, and when I penetrate into these thighs, when I burrow my way in and am inside and move in this interior that is now only tangibly warm and moist, and while doing so I follow her curves with my hands, and perhaps just now catch one more, last impression of her lips, these lips that are curved this way or that, before her mouth is sealed by mine and only our tongues are still there, and everything engulfs me, engulfs us in this feeling, this feeling of pleasure that increases till we go wild, the two naked people, held in an embrace, struggle as one, their bodies intertwined, and small sighs of desire, gasps of breath come from this stranger's throat, and I break out in a sweat that mixes with the sweat of this Ada in our excitement, and all that takes place in this room, and now our senses vanish, and with the vanishing of our senses the last fragments of foreignness float away in a single sound from the throat, or a scream, there's long since been no place anymore for shame or restraint on our part, we don't know one another but are now more ardently alloyed than anyone, because what is exchanged here, what is created in this moment?

And later, with or without cigarettes between their fingers, she can stroke the hair from his forehead, he can stroke the hair from her forehead, with the tenderness of people who have been close friends since the beginning of time. The room remains a room rented by the hour, with this or that bed or basin and scrap of curtain, but now there's a breath or a note, a tint in it, something like a reflection of them that accompanies them in thought as a sort of mood when she, dressed again, her make-up applied again, is all done up and the two of them, no longer standing flat on the floor in their naked feet, but rather in shoes, leave the room and go down the stairs and separate on the street. Ada, ciao Ada, I say, or he says, but that didn't happen in Paris, that was somewhere else or everywhere, I'm starting to talk about the feeling of reserve between people and about this precipitous removal of that reserve, of that plunge into this other thing. In my memory, in my thoughts, the room is pink or pinkish-red, and I think it was in Rome and some time ago.

I no longer know when it began, this absolute craving, this running after women, this obsession, and sometimes I was so obsessed that it seemed to me as if I were intimately acquainted with every individual body part of every woman. And I'm running around with people who are entirely naked, I'm carried along with crowds of people as I drift through the long corridors of the Metro, through the streets, and I can hardly keep myself under control, it's a feeling of happiness, of profound understanding. I can hardly keep myself under control, I say, yes, can hardly keep myself from grabbing at passersby, from reaching out and touching all the rear ends that are waving at me, winking at me though the folds of their jeans, why on earth do we have these preambles, these proprieties, these formalities, come, let's lie down together, I think, or, anyway, the thought crosses my mind as I walk along. And in social settings, when I'm in this state of mind, I would like to say, instead of "pleased to meet you, my name is so and so, I'm this and that, it's a pleasure, nice evening, isn't it," I would like to say "come, let's take our clothes off, come now, no names." This conversation with our hands on the other person's body, this and the other afterward, this plunge head over heels from being reserved into being intertwined, as if this were the only possible way of making oneself understood, the only language on earth, as simple as breaking bread. A feeling of physical understanding, a feeling of happiness, as if I had the magic wand and I feel this swelling and through the swelling this lust for living, this lust to make everything come alive, as if I could awaken everything to life, it's a feeling I also get when I'm writing, when I finally reach the point where I'm not writing, where *it*'s writing itself, an exuberance.

I don't know when that began, don't know if it had something to do with my mother or with my father, but it definitely did have something to do with the fact that they were unapproachable, I felt excluded, solitary, obstinate and lonely, afraid of dying, of death.

Of going numb, I was afraid of that all too often when I was first here in Paris, then I had no desire at all to leave the apartment. I didn't want to go out because I expected myself to work, but the concept of work became increasingly empty, until at last just the word sufficed to set off a panic attack. Work would have meant writing, but what should I write in my boxroom, in this state of emergency. I was cut off from everything, and when I had taken myself out for my morning walk and was back again, staring at the old dove man, I found that I was motionless, buried alive, stiff as a corpse. I had become a boarder, my boarding house was this huge city that no longer enticed or inspired me as it had before, it seemed to me like one of those magnificent, exotic, carnivorous plants that are so fascinating in their fully unfolded splendor, but if you touch them, they roll themselves up and contract to a tiny, unspectacular lump—that's exactly how the city withdrew from me into something untouchable. Since I was starting to lose the habit of daily work, and no longer participated in the working life of the many countless people around me, I had lost all interest in roaming around, I sat in the trap of my boxroom and started listening to my own panic. For a long time, I didn't ask myself if I was unhappy, I just noticed that something wasn't right. I caught myself avoiding my desk, pretending to tidy up the apartment, and spending inordinate lengths of time in the kitchen. Or I went out after all, hurriedly, somewhere, I quickly had to set myself a goal, unless I already had a pretext, such as when I had promised a painter I would have a look at his exhibition, and in order to do so I had to locate Rue de Lille, which branches off Rue des Saint-Pères near the Seine. Afterward, I took the bus to Gare de L'Est and then carried on home on the Metro, but I didn't have anything to eat at home, so I decided to go to the Greek restaurant behind my building on Rue Marcadet. I was the only patron when I arrived, the only person in this charmingly arranged empty room that looked downright inviting with its neatly-set tables and the many individually burning candles on the red tablecloths, the candles were set in bottles that had cataracts of wax around their necks, I had with me a philosopher's manuscript that the painter had given me, it was a nit-picking analysis of his work, about the seeing or imagining of his kaleidoscopic paintings that evoked something like a science-fiction version of paradise, and the philosopher had come to the conclusion that one saw nothing, that is, objectively and with certainty one couldn't recognize anything definite at all in these pictures, the pictures were cleverly devised traps, mousetraps for the imagination, basically just hollow spaces, or something to that effect. I had neither exactly understood his conclusion, nor did I want to, after what the painter had told me about him, I could imagine this thinker quite well, he would have depressed me, not inspired me. A confirmed bachelor between sixty and seventy, an emigrant from Prague, allegedly a blood relation of Kafka's, he had lived in South America for a long time and was now in Southern France as a person without a home or a nationality, eking out an existence rather than living life to the full, he had no feeling at all for art, but was full of theories, said the artist, not without envy, in my mind's eye I saw the gentleman as a sort of nuisance down there in Provence and in the Provençal artists' circles, an argumentative gentleman, heaven knows, I said under my breath. I had just this one manuscript with me, nothing else to read while I waited for my meal in the candlelight that illuminated the many waiting tables, causing them to shimmer. The philosopher lived in a rented apartment in a tiny Provençal nest, he was contemplating writing all sorts of books; and so I had another go at the nit-picking manuscript, and there was Greek folk music playing, a zither recording, the theme from *Zorba* perhaps, it's played in all Greek restaurants, and the rather chubby owner with his hissing, lisping French busied himself at the bar, another customer was sitting there now, chatting with the owner's wife, a corpulent younger woman with glasses, a hard worker who could, when necessary, be surprisingly friendly, a French woman, and there was yet another customer who kept talking on the phone at the end of the counter near the exit, and I drank the retsina and ate the excellent dishes that the owner served up with visible pride, which is why he didn't allow himself to appear amiable, and in between I leafed through the indigestible philosophizing by the Provençal from Prague, then a large group of pretty girls came in with their friends, boyfriends, companions, the restaurant owner led them to a long table and seated them there; I found one of them extraordinarily appealing, she looked me boldly in the eye, once when they were coming in and again when she went past me on her way to the toilet, now I felt even more morose, I asked myself what the owner must be thinking of me. I went out stiffly, I'm moving now in a stiff and contorted manner, I thought, and I trudged back along deserted Rue Marcadet with its partially torn-up sidewalk, in this condition it seemed to be in even worse disrepair than before. I took care to get past Said's unseen, and at home I lay on the sofa because a late movie was about to begin, good timing, I thought, but then it turned out to be Pasolini's *Teorema*, which I'd already seen and didn't want to see again, not now, so I turned off the television and tried to read myself to sleep.

I can't say I was sad, because I wasn't feeling anything, I was probably sad to the extent that I felt almost chloroformed and had become insensitive to pain. I thought about the girl who'd appealed to me at the Greek restaurant and suddenly I felt this desire for a woman. It's like an addiction, I'm like a gambler, I'd bet the shirt off my back to get what I wanted. My horror vacui filled itself up with this desire, it seemed as if I'd have to give up the ghost if I didn't find a woman. So I got up again, ran down the stairs and onto the street. The Chunga Bar on Rue Victor Massé in the 9th arrondissement below Pigalle is one of these establishments that you notice when you're strolling past, because through the window or the half-open door you see a whole row of girls of all skin colors sitting at the bar like birds on a perch. With their generously plunging necklines and short skirts, these partially dressed girls call themselves hostesses. During the day, when not much is going on, they stare out at the street with their painted faces, smoking, and thoughtfully keeping a lookout for customers and clients. The fellow at the door, the tout and if necessary the bouncer, had guided me in, I let it happen, because I was undecided, so I just murmured, it's okay, not necessary, I know my way around. And inside, in the darkened bar that smelled of women's perfume and shimmered with their appearance, I surprised him by asking in a very business-like tone for Cathy. She came out from one of the hookers' hangout corners where the girls were whispering and, sit with me there, she said and pointed to a well-lit table up at the front, a table that was set, where she sat down right away for a meal. Haven't had anything between my teeth since noon, she said, and now it's long past midnight. And now, with slightly affected hand and mouth movements, carefully calculated gestures so that she won't smear the thick make-up on her pretty mouth or get any food on her skintight, expensive dress, she eats little bites of an omelet. I haven't been in town for very long, I say, so I'm just asking to make sure, you do remember me, don't you? No, she says, feigning unfamiliarity between two bites, and then right afterward: how are your books coming along? Then while eating she takes my hand, placing it on her hip, there, put your hand there, she says and keeps on eating. And then she says, with a glance at a tall and quite good-looking lad in a trench coat who's leaning gloomily against the bar, look at him over there, he's been waiting quite a while, he's crazy about me, but I don't like him.

Why, I say, he's quite good-looking. Oh, she says, chewing, he's so . . . I just don't like him, that's all.

And I feel her smooth body through the glittering material of her dress, my hand remembers, there's a familiarity, a feeling of being-on-you in this touch, and now I remember how we used to sit here before, and across from us this old man Cathy called the Papa of them all, she said he came every week and liked to have them nibble behind his ears, that turned him on, she had said, and asked me to dance with her, and we danced over to his table pressed tightly together and stayed in that spot, right under his eyes, he liked that, watching, and she was pleased to do that for him.

Later, I had already said good-bye, but stayed a little while sitting there, Cathy did go up then to the man in the trench coat, after all, she has to work, and while he—from his profile he seemed to be very drunk or maybe just melancholy—started grazing on her cheeks, her hair, her neck with his lips, she winked at me. She let him do everything to her and yet never let me out of her sight.

I like the confidential aspect of such relationships, which by the way are very casual, very lightweight. I like the complicated solidarity, because here, where everything is influenced by venality, the extras, the little votes of confidence, do have the nature of beautifully shining kindness. I've always had this special relationship to so-called loose women, this offhand relationship that also incorporates closeness. When did that begin, I sometimes ask myself.

I've always been surrounded by women, I grew up in a household of women, there was my mother, my sister, my grandmother and great-aunt, and our servant girls; and since we had turned our household into a boarding house, and especially into a boarding house for students, several female boarders always lived with us under the same roof, some of whom strongly appealed to me or at least attracted me. There was one in particular, called Colette, and hardly do I think of her name or speak it aloud than the memory of another person occludes it, of a young man called Gerhard Kummer, obviously the two of them were involved in some way.

Gerhard Kummer was an extremely self-controlled, but also very rebellious young man of not quite twenty. He worked as a proof-reader in a printing business, but aspired to better things. He had grown up in the country and didn't seem to have been in the city long when he moved into our boarding house, a newcomer to the city, green, and as such, he made a great show of dignity, both in his appearance and in his behavior—I think this poseur wanted to give the impression that he was a man of the world. He had the habit of confronting me in the stairwell and involving me in a conversation in a roundabout way by employing strange introductory turns of phrase. He began, for example, with "hm, what I wanted to say was . . ." or "hm, I just had an idea . . ." or "hm, the thought just occurred to me, hm . . ." while he strove to stand there looking very important, I don't know who he was imitating at such moments, he shifted from one foot to the other, and the strangest thing was that while doing so he directed his eyes at my stomach, he sent them circling around like two small beetles at the height of my stomach, which I found very embarrassing, and then, what's more, he avoided opening his mouth while speaking, so his monologues went on and on, always in a strained voice with a nasal twang. At first, I was impatient to the point of being indignant, I couldn't stand his verbiage, and I also took exception to the fact that he seemed to have a very high opinion of himself. Gerhard Kummer read a lot, that was obvious, and one couldn't help but notice it because he liked to lecture and expatiate with a lot of verbal footnotes, which of course didn't make it any easier to listen to him. He read both classical writers and all sorts of books on the occult, the occult in particular interested him. It didn't occur to me that he wasn't just a braggart and a nuisance in the house, a crude sectarian, but that he might be a young man with real problems, a very lonely young person who was trying to make friends, otherwise I wouldn't have been so cold to him. But Gerhard Kummer's attempts to make contact, his long-winded advances to me finally did meet with success, and the reason for that was the arrival of a new female boarder in whom we were both very interested.

The new girl, called Colette, appeared in our apartment late one evening when the dinner table, the *table d'hôtes*, had already been cleared, it was winter, and I saw her negotiating with Mother at the long table under the lamp in the dining room, I happened to surprise them in their negotiations when I looked in quickly as I went past because I heard voices, no, because I became aware of a voice I didn't know.

She had the most catlike eyes I'd ever seen, so lazy and moist, and she smelled strongly of powder and perfume, or of a mixture of powder, perfume, and pure sexuality. Her mouth was wide and full, wide and moistly glistening, and together with her half-closed cat's eyes, that were likewise moistly glistening, and this particular scent, her face made an absolutely erotic impression. She slumped lazily in her chair, only partially present, mentally absent, only physically there, as if she got along in life without thinking, with her body alone.

My mother must have registered the same thing, I could see it in her disapproving, profoundly negative posture; but Colette didn't seem to take offense, she hardly looked my mother in the face, she spoke quietly and sleepily to herself. She got her room and her place in our apartment, our daily routine, our boarding house, we were reliant on rent money in those days, the times were anything but rosy.

It wasn't long before Herr Kummer brought the conversation around to the new girl, and now, from one of the speeches he gave while standing in the stairwell, a speech slowed to interminability by the many redundant and hackneyed phrases he brought out in his strained voice, I found out that he too was interested in the new female boarder in the room next to his. Gerhard Kummer was evidently disturbed by her, in fact, he was all worked up about her, but the main thing he was trying to put into words was the fact that Colette had an extremely active sex life. She had a boyfriend, I knew that much, a showoff in his thirties who made a vital, if not brutal impression; but in addition to him, according to Kummer, there were other gentlemen as well who enjoyed Colette's sexual favors. I was perplexed, less by the fact itself than by the bearer of such knowledge. How could he be so well informed, I wondered, and after considerable beating around the bush he acknowledged that he had witnessed her in the act. Witnessed her in the act? Yes. When Colette had company, he would crouch on the sloping roof outside her window and watch. With that I became more interested in this boarder and detective I had always taken for an unsophisticated person and a moral coward, and as we became more closely acquainted I found out that he walked around on the roofs at night. Possibly the young man's own sexuality was somewhat repressed. In any case, he was curious, a voyeur; he did it both intentionally and deliberately as well as unconsciously, because as it turned out he was also a sleepwalker, neighbors had discovered him one evening or night walking across the roofs and had notified the police. After that, there were conversations with Mother, his relatives were sent for, people discussed what to do, and then one day he didn't come back. Around the same time, he gave up his job as a proofreader, chucked it, as he told me, he wanted to further his education by taking evening courses, he had saved enough money to do so, and much later someone claimed that our former boarder, Herr Gerhard Kummer, had earned his certificate for teaching primary school and had even gotten married, and, right, one could see him now and then arm in arm with his wife, a respectable young married couple going home in a very civilized manner after attending a concert or a lecture, but that was later, in any case, we lost touch with him.

But Colette stayed on. I was in high school and still inexperienced with women, but I was bewitched by her sensuality, I was absolutely crazy about her and was always looking for new pretexts to get close to her. Finally, a certain familiarity developed between us, more a feigned camaraderie than a real one, but under the surface the atmosphere was charged, at least for me. This relationship allowed me not only to remain standing below the door to her room when I called her for dinner or to the phone, but also to go into her room. One evening, as I entered her room under some pretext, I found Colette in a negligee, she was in the midst of some elaborate toilet, and I sensed immediately that she was in a milder, more indulgent mood than usual, much more accessible to me, perhaps her boyfriend had stood her up or left her. We just stood around for a while, I was embarrassed, and she was prevented by my presence from continuing to attend to her personal hygiene, prevented also from going to bed. Then I summoned up my courage and tried to embrace her, it took all my courage to do so, I was somewhat younger than her and certainly less experienced, which was also the reason she'd been able to keep me at bay until then without any difficulty, but on this evening she seemed different, she seemed malleable, in need of love and affection. It's true she evaded my importune attempts to force myself on her, but she did so in a way that just urged me on all the more. One of my awkward attempts turned into a chase around the table and straight across the room until suddenly, I'm not sure if it was on my initiative or under her direction, I fell on the bed together with her and lay full length on top of her. We lay there, the soft Colette, apparently created for nothing but bed, smelling of powder and sexuality, signaling a thousand appeals to my sex from every pore of her flesh, and at the moment compliant as she lay full length under me, and I snuggled up in her flesh, covered her face with kisses, stroked her hair, I did it all with my face as red as a beet, and I was probably panting terribly too, but I did it too long, it went on and on without developing into anything further, and Colette didn't help me, so at last we were exhausted. She took my face in both hands, stroking it as one strokes a child's face, but not a man's, and she pushed me aside and away from her with a motherly sigh. With that, I had missed my only chance, I never got to touch her again, although I tried to get physical with her whenever the opportunity arose, she remained charming, but rejected my advances, she had relegated me to the realm of children and young boys.

I had more luck with petite Oila. She was attending a secretarial school, and in the nights or evenings she visited me in the attic room I was so proud of because I had painted and furnished it myself. I was so proud of it that I had tried several times to do charcoal drawings of it, complete with the cylindrical iron stove and the pictures hanging on the walls, reproductions of Gauguin's paintings of women. We often lay in this small attic room, or, more precisely, on the couch in this room, Oila and I, and in the warmth that the cylindrical oven puffed into the front of the room by the dormer window, and in the colored light of the covered lamps, I was filled with delight when I told myself that a girl was lying there with me, that everything, the entire *set* of everything feminine was collected on my bed, breasts with nipples, stomach and mons veneris, thighs, arms, hands, fingers, fingertips, and nails collected on my bed, offered to me to caress, explore, play with, love, and above it all was Oila's head with her frizzy dark hair and her dark eyes and her mouth that was always in motion, and sometimes her eyes said: do it, do it a little more, do it again! and sometimes: no, not like that! said the eyes that kept watch over the entire position of Oila's beautifully stretched out physical being, but naturally also over me. I liked it, I also liked this attentiveness, this watchfulness of goosegirls who don't let a single one of their darling little goslings get lost or come to any harm.

Oila lay there like an Olympia, or a nude by Modigliani, with her entire young body beautifully spread out, she lay there with her arms folded behind her head and with her budding breasts tilting to the right or left and with her frizzy triangle and with her supervising eyes continuously encouraging me and spurring me on, and then again signaling that it was time to stop.

I was blissful and serious and devoted to our play and I suspected that something indescribably more intense lay waiting for me there, an entranceway, and I whispered, I'll go in search of it, I'll gain entrance, I'll seek it, cost what it may, I will find it.

I am often irresistibly aware of this allure of a woman, but there's a reverent veneration of beauty, even an adoration in this feeling of equating beauty with a woman's body, with the line of her back, this indentation leading down to her splendidly spreading bottom and the smooth casting of her legs—an ancient, an archaic veneration. And immediately afterward the maddest desire: to dive into these splendors. Then comes the obsession with getting closer to each other until our limbs are joined, until we put aside our fear and are conversing with nothing but "our hands on the other person's body" and carrying on until we are intertwined, until our senses disappear and fade away. Hallucinations, obsessions. And sometimes it seemed to be the only promise of comfort, the only means of clinging to life when I feared I would become desolate in the seclusion of my boxroom, in my horror vacui, that was it: the thought of the female continent and of conquering it were one and the same, *one* with the hope of being saved from a fear that was boring itself into my brain from somewhere down below, and I measured the degree of my isolation, of my longing for lost protection, of my anxiety, by the intensity of my wishful thinking. But sometimes I feel as if I could sculpt bread out of stone, I feel something effervescent, like omnipotence. And then again something like writing poetry and praying.

Writing poetry. I think that in my case the erotic awareness of life, or, rather, its awakening coincided with the awakening of my urge to write; the two occurred simultaneously in a wave of sensuality, in a corresponding confusion of my senses. I was in my boyhood, going through puberty, and sometimes I skipped school just to escape all the talking there, to be able to be alone with myself. Every few weeks I had the irresistible urge to be alone like that, then I let down the green Venetian blinds at the window and lay down to dream. Especially in the spring, the summer, or Indian summer, green filtered light flowed in through the gaps in the Venetian blinds, I lay as if in a greenhouse, lay there and let myself drift away in erotic fantasies. My erotic fantasizing was not simply in my head or imagination, it was a general surge of pleasure, it was a tugging and buildup, I played with my penis, I masturbated, and then I fell into a sort of unconsciousness in which images or inchoate images, images that had not yet taken final shape began to appear in outline, and were then accentuated, I floated through corridors of images, they weren't erotic images, they were images of states of happiness, and these states of happiness were always related to the happiness of gardens or in gardens, with the filtered green sunlight, small arcs

of light, with perceptions, perceptions of beauty, beauty, with paradise? And once, when I was in this state, sentences crossed my vision
for the first time, or I saw myself lying there and heard something
talking in me, something breathless, but not confused, just sentence
after sentence, it ran on for pages, out of me, or in front of me, I
could hear it, even read it, it all came to me with the greatest clarity
and lucidity, and I lay there and listened with breathless attention to
the sentences that ran out of me and flowed away before my eyes, I
listened to them and saw them, and could do nothing for or against
it, just lie there, listen, see. That went on until I was exhausted and
fell asleep. Afterward I had only a vague memory of it, as of a dream.
Although I knew for sure that I had heard myself speak and had seen
myself speak, for a long time, and as if it were being dictated to me, I
could not reproduce what had overcome me after I woke up. I could
only awaken the entire state in me again.

Just as I can recall the speaking and speaking in sentences, speaking in pages running through me at the onset of puberty, I experienced the same sensation later when I was making love, when
immediately after the orgasm I would dive away into a wholly visual
reality, I would slip into pictures, into scenes I could observe. Once I
saw myself sneaking through undergrowth, I forced my way through
undergrowth that was wet from the rain and into a forest, I saw and
felt the heavy wet branches against my face, my cheeks, I smelled
the slightly bitter scent of the wet branches, the pungency of this
scent, the harshness of their cold, hard touch, I thrashed my way
deeper into the woods, and then I saw a tree in front of me, it stood
in a clearing, alone, and it started to twitch and shake itself, as if it
wanted to double up with laughter, as if it enjoyed shaking itself, it
looked as if it were dancing. I saw that and thought, a twitching tree
shaking itself when there's no wind at all? I didn't even know that a
tree could move of its own will, let alone dance, I thought, as I lay
beside the woman and our relaxed limbs were touching and we drew
light breaths together. It was the clearest form of seeing or, better,

visualizing, as no word can ever conjure it up, express it, or make it perceptible, it was the unattainable vision, it was overwhelming, and I lay in a great state of innocence, watching the image.

I think it was the erotic sense of simply being alive that enticed and directed me into daydreaming. It's a preliminary stage of visualization, imagination, and has to do with the creation of another, second reality, another life—and yet, early on, I was more than a little ashamed of the inwardness that gave rise to this other reality.

When I was still quite young, I had my own bicycle, a so-called semi-racer, to which I was really attached. On this bicycle, I liked to whiz and speed down through Bremgartenwald, through the forest to the lake, Wolensee, where for fifty centimes I could rent a boat, a flat-bottomed punt, a fishing boat, in which I could drift around on the lake all afternoon when I had the day off. On the lake there were always several real fishing boats with real fishermen, they were motionless on the usually calm water as if rooted to the bottom, now and then one of the fishermen reeled in one of his lines, now and then he threw a line out, I could see the bobber bouncing around, and in the evenings they beat the fish to death, the ones they had caught, to me it sounded like the threshing of reapers, it didn't sound like killing at all, it was a sound of peace, like church bells ringing in the evening, a sound from olden times. I did nothing of the sort, I actually did nothing whatever in or with my boat, I dreamed, that is, I imagined that I wasn't on Wolensee, but rather in a Norwegian fjord or up in Michigan, a trapper. The lake wasn't a real lake, just a wider section of the Aare, although it has the German word for lake in its name. There were whole fields of reeds in the middle of it, real sandbars, and along the shore there were huts on posts that belonged to the fishermen, and all around the forest came down right to the water's edge, making the lake dark, it was a forest lake, I rowed through the patches of reeds, upstream, and sometimes I let myself drift for a long time; or I landed, acted out difficult landings for myself and real scenes of going ashore, that was breaking new ground, adventurous, full of promise, I secretly re-experienced other lives, lives I had read about or imagined to myself, they always involved hard, real, adventurous living, never idle hours, sports, or relaxation. Wolensee was my place for thoughts, wishes, and longings in which I anticipated life, life that wasn't taking place on the street where I lived, Berner Länggasse, that street which descended on me regularly with its deadly dreariness. What I was playacting there was an alternative life, and this life took place in my imagination in the big wide world I so longed to see, just as I constantly yearned for love, for amorous adventures. On that lake, I composed my first and only poem, I composed it "in the presence of nature," and I was very astonished and really overwhelmed that it had arisen in me as if by itself. When I had maneuvered the punt to the dock in the evening and tied it up securely and got on my bicycle to ride home, then it was as if I was returning home from work, from a day's labor, I was carrying a sort of booty or harvest home with me. At least I was carrying the smell of brackish water and of reeds, the smell of earth and rain on my clothes. The lake was a place of anticipation and waiting, I waited there for my life to begin, the life that would welcome me once I had finished school. It should be a life as large as possible, full of the power of the real world.

For a while, for several years, I was always on my bicycle, or so it seems to me now, I could even stand up while riding it, which was done by continually turning the front wheel from left to right, twisting it, keeping it in motion, and at the same time balancing like an acrobat over the seat, I remember standing together with other schoolboys in the same manner and getting pointers from them, each of us twisting and turning on his bicycle like a contortionist. The bicycle also served as a vehicle for getting to school, and several times I took part in longer bicycle trips, but that's not important, for our purposes, what counts here is just the bicycle trip I went on with Lara.

With Lara, I rode from Bern to Thunersee, Lake Thun, to Oberhofen, we rode through the summer, the summer grew in toward both sides of the road from the yellow cornfields, it hummed in the sleepy air, it hummed in the heat that made the spokes of our wheels flash, we had this entire summer to ourselves, it was all for us, we bent over our bicycles with our hot faces and we bent beaming toward each other, our skin was soft and smelled like calfskin, we were heated up not just by the summer and by the exertion of pedaling, but also by the excitement, we loved each other, and when we lay in the grass for a rest, we tussled, rolled around, hugged, kissed each other in our young summer bodies, whose calfskin smell mixed with the rich, slightly bitter, wonderful smell of grass. Once we were lying in a park and only then noticed that it was a graveyard, a graveyard for fallen soldiers, I think it was an American one, we embraced each other above the dead.

At that time I wore a special pair of sunglasses that covered the upper half of my face as if to disguise me, so I felt I was incognito, or at least sheltered, when I waited for Lara outside the iron gate of the girls' school, I waited on my bicycle, supporting myself with one leg, and saw all the girls come swarming out, approaching me in chattering groups, and I kept a lookout for her from behind the mask of my sunglasses, I didn't even really know if I liked her, I couldn't ask myself that question, because I was dependent on our being in love, dependent on this atmosphere as if it were a drug, that's why I was dependent on her, whether I wanted to be or not. I couldn't be without either. That's why I wore the sunglasses.

I remember the asphalt as being very pale, light and pale, the course of my life was not yet clear to me, and perhaps that's why the asphalt was so pale and light, pale with expectation, light and empty from the pent-up feelings of expectation in me, my expectations of life. But now I was waiting for Lara, and then she came, she separated from a group and came toward me very quickly, perhaps a little coyly, because she had to be aware of how very much the other girls pretended that they didn't see anything and didn't know anything and made for the gate with such an exaggerated display of being carefree. Because of that, Lara seemed a little inhibited, but there was also something else that expressed itself in her posture, it showed in the way she separated from the group of girls and came running over to me by herself: a rare dignity, a woman's dignity. It was the burden of love, I say, this weight, this seriousness. A composure that included the danger of being hurt, of being misused, of pain. In that, she was far ahead of me, she was—she was *totally* involved, whereas I was holding something back in myself, as if I wanted to keep myself for something greater, something more beautiful, later on.

Lara came up to me with this composure, this special sense of fulfillment, we greeted each other shyly, and then we took off, out of the range of vision of the other schoolgirls, the witnesses. We walked along side by side, with me pushing my bicycle, and at every opportunity we pressed against each other, lusting insatiably for each other. But there was always this seriousness about her, this wholeness that was so superior to what I had to offer.

Lara had brown skin, brown eyes, and brown hair, she was seventeen, she could have come from Northern Italy or from South Tyrol. I met her at a party, it was a class of girls from a commercial college who had invited my class for whatever reason. Lara was not the most beautiful, but she was the most mature, she was also the most foreign. She was probably Swiss, like the rest of us, but she had come from another country, from a warzone, to Bern, she had experienced war, and she didn't live with her parents, but with relatives. She had this different background, this secret; a restraint, that made her seem like an adult among children. After a sort of preliminary round, I was her dancing partner, then her partner for the evening, she had become mine, and we danced without banter and without silly remarks right into this being in love, this drunken, sadly beautiful space. I'd hardly had time to look at her, I didn't know what she was like or who she was or even if I liked her, and already I was in this giddy state.

I picked her up every day from school, we went for a walk, and once she went with me to my attic room, and now I remember that she asked me not to go too far, that she asked me to be careful. I lay with her on the couch, we were all aglow, but it wasn't the same as with Oila, who instructed me and simultaneously supervised me, in fact it was much more appealing: Lara asked me with hesitation and whispering to act *for her*, left to herself she wouldn't have been able to exercise restraint, she would have had to give her all right away, she was passionate to go all the way, to put her soul into it, she was ready for love. I was attracted by her skin, I surrendered myself to her skin, her proximity made me drunk, and I dwelt on this drunkenness, this blissful state, behind my sunglasses and also at school, I just wanted to foster and preserve this state, aside from that, I dreamed of the time soon approaching when I would graduate from school. I also spoke frequently about my future, and accordingly of years of travel, campaigns of conquest, the daring intentions I had, the paths I would take, all of which had to lead into the wide world. The future stood large before me, like a forcibly opened barn door, and now it occurs to me that the reason why the bicycle trip we took together to Lake Thun is so ethereal in my memory, why I see it before a gleaming gold background in my mind's eye, and why it has remained like that, is because even at that time, when we undertook it, it was already too beautiful and probably in some way elegiac and not entirely real. It was the last trip through childhood, the wide world of summer still belonged to us, just as back then the whole landscape had belonged to us like an endless garden, but we were in the process of leaving this land, the summer seemed so great to me because it was also created by this feeling of love, by this heartbeat, it pulsated with that feeling of intoxication. I rode my bicycle from Bern to Lake Thun, but at the same time I was being propelled along, driven by this hunger for life and blinded by thoughts of a future that took place in a novel, a romantic novel, in my mind.

By the way, I also didn't know exactly who we were riding to meet. Lara had spoken about visiting an uncle, and I had some unclear notion of a poor refugee or emigrant, of someone who had found a hiding place, and now we stopped in front of a huge hotel of the noblest design, in which people like Tolstoy might have stayed, and her uncle introduced himself as the owner. We drank tea by the billowing drapes on one of the countless balconies, we sat in this humming orange-filtered summer light, in this warm partial shade, her uncle was a tall, cultured, middle-aged man, and his speech was very quietly tired, polite, and discreet, he might as well have been part of the scenery, and a waiter dressed in white, a servant, came and went all the while, no less a bit of set dressing.

Shortly afterward, I traveled to Paris to spend the holidays with my aunt, at that time she lived below Pigalle, and when I took the dog out for his evening walk, the dog at that time was called Tobe, I breathed in the smell of the trash cans in the courtyard with the conspiratorial consent of this accomplice, with an inappropriate exuberance, the garbage smelled different here than it did in Bern, it smelled a little of the Metro, just as the courtyard smelled a little like Javel water or Javex, the trash cans and the courtyard smelled of Paris, I was in Paris, I could take the dog out for a walk, just like all the others took their dogs out for walks, I was one of them, I was part of Paris, and on Avenue Trudaine, in the shadow of its long walls with the few bistros and cafés built out onto the wide sidewalk, I formulated little descriptive phrases that were still without any real context and therefore probably didn't make sense, from every meter of asphalt I sensed and absorbed the entire magnificence of this city, and when my aunt set the table for our late dinner and put the long loaf of bread beside the cutlery, I gazed in wonder at this staff as if it were a relic or a covenant. I pledged allegiance to the bread and the smell of the trash cans and to the gurgling of the water in the gutter, I clung to these common things that for me were Paris or stood for Paris, my love of the world clung to this pledge, my dream kept a firm hold on it.

I was in Paris and reveling in new impressions, but under the surface I began to worry about my Lara, whom I had left behind, I felt my confidence crumbling, didn't know why, and when I got back from my holidays and phoned her home, a stranger's voice asked me not to call again, and when I finally saw Lara again, she was short with me and asked me to leave her alone. I had always spoken of my future, of plans that did not include her in any way. I only wanted to experience LOVE with her and excluded her as a person. She had been far ahead of me with her readiness, she must have seen through my conflict, my selfishness, she had finally made her decision during the time I was in Paris, she had sorted things out in her own mind, and now she held firmly to her decision.

When I first went to Paris, the train got in at midnight or later, and my aunt met me at Gare de l'Est. We took a taxi to Pigalle and then walked the short distance to her building. I didn't know what nightlife was, I had never experienced it, now I was overwhelmed, devoured by nightlife. The streets shimmered in the reflections of the most diverse lighting, such as the colored neon signs, the neon lettering and decorative lights of all the bars and night spots, restaurants and shops, the doors of the bars opened and shut like pumps, emitting torrents of music, the boom of loudspeakers, quarrelling, talking, and people. Outside the bars, half-undressed girls, hostesses, prostitutes twitched and turned to the beat of all kinds of music, and walking past all of that were masses of people, lechers, pleasure-seekers; there were hookers and striptease-dancers slipping past who would cross the street quickly or disappear with a guy into the entranceway of a sleazy hotel, and then there were the doormen too. The night had been turned into a sparkling, humming, booming, into a madly warming and exciting night*life*, into a Bengalese Orcus, no expense had been spared, everything could be had here, all kinds of food and drink, flowers and drugs, revolvers, people, it was a night market, a pleasure market, a human market, the craving for pleasure blazed out of every bar door, it twitched in the twitching movements of the prostitutes in the doorways and was disreputably silent in the made-up faces of the whores leaning outside the hotel entranceways, in their inviting expressions and hips, I went along beside my petite aunt through this midnight funfair, in a wave of perfume and joie de vivre, past restaurants, through whose brightly-lit windows one saw the boisterous patrons slurping oysters and devouring sauerkraut, I pushed my way through this surging crowd, the stream of strolling people was so dense that I thought I could walk or push my way through on their heads, I was dazed and ecstatic and at the same time my sexual desire was aroused a thousandfold.

When I strolled along Boulevard de Rochechouart with my aunt in the coming days, I saw night become day and then night again. We sat on the patio of a café as if alongside the stream of life, we sat on the shore, on a shore that stretched for kilometers in fantastic animation, door to door, bar to bar, light to light, and we looked at this incessant human procession that pushed past us, a procession of nighttime strollers greedy for life, greedy for experience, with many tourists among them, all of them had this hungry, enraptured look, they walked as if in a trance, but also like convicts, like people chained together, they were at the mercy of the nightly miracle, the confusing range of special offers, they walked along with the slow, laborious movements of the mystified, they couldn't stand still at all, they pushed themselves along and were pushed by others, pushed past our glances, flooded by all these stimuli, the stimuli of lights, temptations, the stimuli of women, the temptations to sin, they went past the inexhaustible attractions, they swam, they went under, they flowed past as if underwater. And between them the street vendors, some with carpets over their shoulders, Arabs and Afro-French, others with indecent cards that they showed secretively, touts, pimps, pushers, flower girls, graphic artists who promised to finish a portrait or a silhouette in no time, white-slave traders, everything, and again the procession of these armies of slaves, captives, blinded, hypnotized. And everything dipped in the lights and in the provocative cacophony of the music streaming forth from a thousand doors.

When I took the dog out the next day, I didn't recognize the streets, they seemed tired to me, like a face without make-up, ravaged, gray, but they soon recovered, and by late morning I found the whores again at their street corners and outside the hotels. If a man passed by, they nodded to him or mimed an invitation some other way, they rang all the changes on "seductive," on "attractive," all kinds of women there in the midst of the daily bustle, they drew attention to themselves by standing there, like sentries, even before one had really seen them, I caught my breath whenever I passed close to them. I thought, life here never stops, a mysterious promise seemed to wave at me from all the walls and doorways, the city seemed full to the brim with an inexhaustible supply of temptation, and for me the greatest temptation of all, the most exciting, somehow the most human, the most sensible, were the girls who lined the streets and entranceways day and night, who assumed their posts, these gatekeepers, these women who bring about an armistice through sex, hetaeras, nixies, sirens, it was calming and very pleasant to know that *this* table would always be set in Paris, so many women ready to receive you, so many gateways into the secret, into adventure, into temptation, no: into life! It was as if one could be continually brought into the world anew by women, or else thrown into the ocean, thrown out. Since I had discovered *this* promise of the city, I vowed and hoped that I would try all gateways, I would attempt to live forever.

"Many men might have killed themselves because of their desire for women if there weren't any prostitutes. Whores helped me after my first separation. I loved my wife immeasurably. She was so pretty that I couldn't sleep peacefully at night when I thought of being without her. The only thing that helped was another woman. You can't just go out and find a decent woman who will spend the night with you. You find whores, beautiful, wonderfully beautiful young girls.

It costs you a few hundred dollars, they stay four or five days and help you get over the sickness. When you have another woman, you realize that you won't die. Such a whore has an important job. How many men are saved by whores. Whores were sent to Jesus . . ." and so on, said Muhammad Ali alias Cassius Clay in an interview (well, I'm paraphrasing from a translation of an interview that he presumably gave, at some point . . .).

I set aside this newspaper clipping once upon a time, and now I've come across it in my boxroom. When you have another woman, you realize that you won't die, says Ali, and I think the same way he does—to die, wither, pass away, take your own life, those are my words, it's exactly the same way for me, especially since I've been so godforsaken and alone here in Paris.

By the way, my dear friend Beat, on one of his recent visits, expressed the opinion that I needed to look for or take or get myself a girlfriend. As if one could just go out and do that. He said: you need a girlfriend, my dear fellow, you're in need of constant female companionship, of someone who waits for you, someone with whom you can share your feelings, your expectations for a pleasant evening, and with whom you can satisfy your desire to be a stallion; you need more than the occasional visit to these *maisons de rendez-vous*, you need a relationship.

But I can't even begin to think of that, let alone wish for it, there's simply no available space in me, the space in question is already taken, doubly taken. Really, Beat, I say, you ought to know that. You must know how much damage ending a marriage can cause. And that's why I've come here, because my marriage broke up. Of course, there was this apartment of my aunt's, this means of escape, but it's a bachelor pad, a place of refuge, a little place where I can lick my wounds, and I still feel really wounded, as you know, I say to Beat.

Now you're exaggerating, he says, *you're* the one who destroyed your marriage, which everyone considered an enviable, indeed warm and successful marriage, *you're* the one who wanted to get out of it.

You fell head over heels in love with this other girl who made you crazy, but didn't accept you, if I understand correctly, says Beat, are you actually a masochist by profession? You can forget the girl, if she doesn't come here of her own accord, and soon, just forget her, he says, and forget your marriage too, forget them both. Find yourself a girlfriend, she can be a barmaid or, even better, a cashier in a department store, go into the department stores and keep a lookout for a pretty cashier, for one who doesn't want to get married right away, for a "sensuous" one who'd like to get some experience first before she starts thinking of having children, a pretty, cheeky cashier, one who's bored at the checkout and in her dreary attic room and with the few egoistic guys she's met until now, who all go to the same sort of bars and have the same sort of buddies, a girl you can spoil a little and train to spoil you, that sort of girl, says Beat.

Now I think *disasters*. Here in my boxroom, I think of the many disasters, I think of my wife's face petrified with pain, it suddenly changed into this cold, arrogant mask with a pointed chin, yes, her beloved face solidified into this mask after I had spoken with her about that other amorous encounter, and in that split second it must have become clear to her that everything that had joined us together and sustained us for so long had been destroyed forever. Now she has this arrogant face that also seems somehow simpleminded, a face has to look simpleminded to show contempt, the face of a Foolish Virgin, I thought, after the long silence that followed my confession, so that I thought I could hear all the sounds of the water and heating pipes, and neither one of us moved in that pipe-silence. After that, we let ourselves be washed away by our tears. No, I don't like to think of the ensuing arguments, the nightly discussions, in which each of us was the other's orderly and good Samaritan, plying ourselves with alcohol. We were swimming in alcohol, we kept reaching for the bottles of wine, we went out to buy more at all hours of the day and night, we always sat together at this negotiation table, faced with our broken marriage, emptying the bottles and filling the ashtrays.

But the worst disasters are of another kind. They're turns of speech that suddenly besiege me, phrases from our private language, the argot that developed between us after all that time, and when I think them or whisper them here, it sounds like blasphemy. Those phrases are the most painful memories, and I'm waiting for them to be extinguished from my mind. What should I do now with this language for two that has become superfluous, that now falls into a void? The orphaned words, the outcast, betrayed language that used to mean home, where should I send it?

You'll forget it, says Beat, after all, you can't have everything, he says. I know he's just saying that to have something to say and to move the conversation along, at least away from this sore point.

Disasters, I think. Disasters—an old word, a beautiful word. But disasters also come from others, I'm caught between two fires, Beat, between the devil and the deep blue sea, I add—I picked up that turn of phrase recently in a bar, of course in French. *Entre deux feux* is what I heard there, people were talking about a love affair, a love triangle.

I can't forget the Other Woman, I say to Beat. I'd like to, but I can't. It's as if I'm in a waiting room here, I can't believe that something that was so intense that it cost me my marriage was merely a product of my imagination. I've been poisoned by this other love, I say, I'm suffering from love poisoning, Beat, I'm waiting.

There are evenings I spend rearranging the apartment, taking care of correspondence, washing the dishes, just to keep myself away from the telephone. I want to prevent myself from dialing that transatlantic number whose ringing or beeping would bring *her*, that is, this other voice onto the line, and with her voice would come her face, the other face that's poisoned me, but I don't do it, I wrestle with myself not to do it, and why? Because I'm afraid. This voice would then come to me through the telephone line across the great ocean and would be here with me in my boxroom, would be alive here and would be a mouth, a face, and I'm afraid a word or even just an intonation, a timbre in this voice, could injure me, worse: *disown me. And leave me without hope here* in this waiting room. Women, my God, women—! says Beat. You're having a midlife crisis, throw yourself into your writing. How should I write in my current state of mind, I say to Beat. I'm being scorched by these two damned fires, I'm not free, I'm blinded. If only I had my ticket, my incentive, my marching orders.

There's your material: Between the devil and the deep blue sea. Write yourself free, he says.

Even better, call it *My Year of Love*. But I can't see my way through. After all, I'm just the innkeeper of my life, and what does an innkeeper know about what goes on in his inn? What I mean by marching orders, by incentive, is that I haven't yet reached the state in which I'll have had enough of it. If only I were at the point where I could move the carriage of my typewriter and take it for walks and send everything away in columns and caravans of words! But in order to do so, I need my ticket. I'm in this waiting room, I'm waiting.

If Beat knew how long it takes before the things kept in the hump of my traveling camel have been sufficiently shaken and fermented, that is, well enough digested so that finally, years later, surfacing as vivid subject matter, as a *contemplation*—or memory?—and can be put into images or coughed up . . . If you knew, I say to Beat. I'm still just the innkeeper, do you understand? I can't see my way through, I'm blind, I can't tap beer anywhere. I have to wait.

That's all Greek to me. You're a philanderer. Come on, let's get out of here. Let's grab a bite to eat, says Beat.

Just now the old dove man has started making a fuss again. Without his old wife he'd have nothing to make a fuss about: that's one of those love-hate relationships, says Beat. They never go out of business.

What grounds do I have to be so opposed to the dove man, what can I have against him, I wonder, after all, over time he's become a real point of reference. We've never yet actually approached each other, never yet had verbal contact, although he's recently started yelling to one of the other tenants who lives on the floor above me, they converse from window to window. The whole thing started with my fellow tenant, a tiny old man who nevertheless seems quite tenacious, a new renter, I meet him in the stairwell, where the tenants generally neither greet nor speak to each other, they go silently past each other, that is, they pause on the wider landings and wait to let whoever is climbing or descending the stairs go past them, as if to avoid a collision, as if there were too little room on the stairs for two people to get past each other, but it's not that, it's a sort of fear of contact, the desire to keep one's distance, it's mistrust. Well, the new man, a short fellow who seems sinewy and tough, who rather resembles the bicycle dealer on our street, recently let me go past him with the following observation: just run on up, I get out of breath climbing the stairs, one just isn't the same person one used to be, and other such sayings, but then, when I was already several steps above him, I heard the remark: it's just not easy to find one's way when one's lost one's mother. I thought I hadn't heard him correctly, because the new tenant must have been long since past retirement age, but the concierge, that woman who, when she isn't drunk, is always grumpy, always smoking, this rather curt, unfeeling person, said to me *en passant* with a hint of sympathy, first the new tenant lost his wife, then he moved in with his mother, who was as old as the hills—back to his mother's breast when he was already a pensioner!—and when she died shortly afterward he took an apartment here. Sometimes I see him looking out his kitchen window onto the front courtyard with a face that clearly shows he's been crying, he cries, the old man, he cries because he's so lonely.

But now he's hit it off with the old dove man, and in the afternoons I see and hear the two of them talking with each other, it's mainly boasting bellowed from window to window, but since then I also know why my old dove man does nothing but sit around, he seems to be really sick, he has leg problems, even if he can still stand up and go out now and then, he must experience, is experiencing a lot of pain nonetheless. As far as their illnesses and afflictions are concerned, they've shouted everything to each other in minute detail, including the remedies they take for them, then they've gone on to talk about everything else under the sun, I still have to verify some of it. It's strange to see how my old dove man behaves when he's sitting sideways like that at his wide-open window, conferring with his new chum and simultaneously watching the one dove that's always eating to make sure she has nothing against this change in their routine. Sometimes he looks at the bird with an almost adoring grimace, then again with a conspiratorial grin, usually though with a pure ex-voto face, while the other man is shouting across at him; perhaps he regrets the fact that his dove life, his exclusive focus on that life-form, has now been devalued by this daily talk.

I think: other people have a dog or a cat or a canary, he has this favorite dove that he spoils and would like to protect from the other greedy doves, that's his right, he's a pensioner and already over seventy, as I now know, so why do I take such exception to him? In any case, the dove man has seemed much more human to me of late, which certainly has something to do with his conversations with the new tenant. They started off with their afflictions, then went on to compare their present state with the way they used to be, when they were still young men, back then they often stayed up all night, just wasting time, of course they worked hard too, and were certainly different from these wimps today, these eunuchs, but so what, they say, it's all the same to them now, soon they'll croak, they're already sick.

I get the impression that the dove man's wife doesn't like to see their developing friendship. Several times now she's cut short one of these afternoon conversations from window to window across the courtyard by picking a fight with her husband, going so far as to shut the window.

They're held together by hatred, said Beat. Maybe he just said it without thinking very much about it, but *I* think this apparent hatred, this nagging, could on the contrary be a rather shameful expression of love, in fact I often think, once I've formed an impression, especially about relationships, that the opposite of whatever conclusion I've come to could just as well be true. I don't know where it comes from, I'm almost pathologically cautious about judgments that have become so-called certainties, not only is something in me constantly weighing in on the opposite side of whatever I've assumed, but also I'm always prepared to discover the most terrible things imaginable, the most terrible revelations.

I say, one can't know for sure, Beat, in fact, one can't know anything about couples, not even they themselves, the people in question, the married couples, those who've been forged together, can know it—what does the innkeeper know of what's going on in his inn?

And I tell him about my Uncle Alois, my mother's brother, who used to impress me when I was a kid, when he would call out, particularly after a good meal: now I'm game for anything again. He had several such turns of speech at his disposal, he also said, when the talk was of a criminal known throughout the city: then there's only one thing to do, first you punch him in the gut, then you follow up with a hook to the chin, and he'll collapse like a sack of flour. And as he said that, my Uncle Alois had this beaming smile, just like an American movie star, a toothpaste-ad smile, he did have very beautiful, pearly white, and even teeth, and his hair was beautifully waved, but otherwise there was nothing about him like a film hero, in fact nothing like a hero at all, he was bonhomie personified, a respectable businessman with a small pharmaceutical business in the country, and every Wednesday he came to our place in Bern, he came both for business as well as for selfless higher purposes, as a secondary occupation he was a preacher, a preacher in a congregation, led by him, of the global Pentecostal movement, if I'm not mistaken, the congregation, consisting mainly of poor people, the majority of them maidservants, old widows, or old maids, paid him, I believe, for his trip there and back, in addition to reimbursing his expenses, and they did so by taking up collections that made life very comfortable for my uncle, whom we also referred to as the "handsome" uncle or the "handsomely rewarded" uncle. He was really well off, he always drove up in this huge American car, and all the female simpletons in his congregation probably loved this smiling, good-looking man a good deal, I always had the suspicion that at those assemblies, which were held in the hall of an inn, there was something like veneration for a bridegroom involved, something sexual that was suppressed. When my uncle was ardently praying and calling upon God with his insatiable grumbling and groaning, reciting his words with sounds of pain mixed with ecstasy, so that his followers groaned along with him, rolling their eyes, this finale of his in the rented parish hall always made me feel sick to my stomach. Without question, my uncle was the shepherd and bridegroom of this congregation comprised primarily of women, and they proved their loyalty to him and dependence on him with cash from the collection that closed out their meetings, just as they did by falling into their atrocious speaking in tongues while praying with him. For my uncle, the Wednesday evening assembly was probably rewarding not only from the business standpoint, but also from the standpoint of his male vanity. At lunchtime, he came to our house, that is, he came to his sister's, our mother's, just to check on us a little, but also to stuff his face, and when he had eaten his fill and was feeling satisfied, he would yawn, give me that special look from the side, and call out the words I could never fully understand: now I'm game for anything again. After the assembly, he drove home through the dark night, with the collection money, in his streamlined American car.

Uncle Alois was not only the rich, handsome uncle with the winning ladies'-man smile, he was also the best husband on earth. And indeed, people thought that he and his wife, our Aunt Rudolfine, would be in love with each other forever, were an eternally cooing couple, whenever people saw them together he couldn't resist pawing her over as demonstratively as possible, while she fended him off with feigned prudishness, mischievous eyes darting left and right, pleading for understanding. And also, when he visited us on Wednesdays, or ate at our table, his favorite topic of conversation was all the things he had bought for his better half, he could also go on at length about his planned weekend pilgrimages to take Rudolfine to four-star restaurants, he liked to talk about his own generosity, which was based of course on his solvency, which is why his relatives thought he was an incorrigible showoff and cock of the walk who simply smothered his wife with care and attention. When he was at our place, he went on and on about his obsession with spoiling his wife, which was embarrassing not only because my mother, his sister, was a widow living in straitened circumstances, but also because, other than with his appetite and his self-satisfaction, he was incapable of showing her the least brotherly affection.

This successful uncle of ours, Uncle Alois, took early retirement from his business life, he wasn't yet sixty when he sold his pharmaceutical business and his house, at a profit, as he emphasized, in order to build an English country house in a select location, where he intended to spend many carefree years in the company of his beloved wife, who had remained youthful, if a little more grandiose around the hips, but this plan was then unfortunately thwarted by a higher power. The house had already been finished, but the garden was still just a sketch, and our rich, handsome Uncle Alois, prematurely freed from his life of hard work as a businessman, as well as from his self-sacrificing life as a sectarian preacher and as a driver of an American car, was working in this not-yet-completed showpiece of a flower garden when he was struck down, right out of the blue and without any advance warning, was hit by a stroke that paralyzed him and robbed him of his speech. From that point on, Uncle Alois was mute, that is, the only word he was able to mumble, the word he had known how to pronounce so captivatingly to the sisters of his sect and to groan out to his God, the only word that now escaped his lips, that remained with him was YES, in his misfortune he had been turned into a sickly yes-man. I was already grown up at the time and visited my uncle in the hospital, where he sat grimly threatening in an armchair, constantly fiddling with the cane in his hands, and whenever I approached him with any noncommittal words of consolation, such as "you'll get better again, Uncle Alois," horrified by the change that had come over him, horrified that my handsome, rich uncle had turned into this heap of a hospital inmate with his dark stare, he would mumbled his "yes yes," which sounded awful to my ears, it was a total transformation, it left him stiff and mute, and on such occasions, whenever our Aunt Rudolfine came in the door, the wife he had spoiled all his life, the wife he had idolized, upon whom he had lavished so many loving words, cooing like a dove, Alois reached for his cane, raised it threateningly with an almost Old Testament gesture and aimed it at the woman entering the room, pure hatred in his face, whereupon he mumbled his "yes yes" and with eloquently wide eyes sought to meet the gaze of his male visitor, as if he wanted to reveal something terrible to him. Now Aunt Rudolfine had also developed a hard, furious expression, she had become a rich but caustic prospective widow, and when the hospital physician suggested that a skilled worker be engaged for the purpose of speech therapy, and that it was as good as certain that my uncle would regain at least partial ability to speak, actually it could be guaranteed with good treatment, she answered with an irreversible NO, she did not want him to receive any additional treatment, and anyway it was too expensive. My mother, Alois's sister, wept sincerely and uncontrollably over her unfortunate brother, and she visited him loyally and untiringly in his sad room.

Uncle Alois belonged to a long series of disappointing father figures for me, there was no replacement father for me in my childhood, I was surrounded by men whose talk was just empty words, who were efficient businessmen for a while, if efficiency can be measured by material success, after which they became bedridden or worn out before their time, all of them, as it seemed to me, were living a sort of lie, and it was probably this lifelong illusion that had puffed up my Uncle Alois to such an extent that something ripped in his brain, until the lie burst, along with his fairy tale of marital bliss and the perfect marriage, and what remained behind was this heap of a person with the dark glare and the immense hatred for his better half, who not only left him in the lurch once he was in trouble, but even gloated over his misfortune. I hadn't liked this Uncle Alois from the start because his behavior toward his sister, my mother, was so cold and merciless, even though he knew how to groan so profoundly to his God. Uncle Alois would have liked to see my mother take my sister and me out of the academic stream and put us into simple vocational apprenticeships after my father died. Now it's all over with the academic high school and the conservatory, he informed my mother, people who have no money should go out and work, not study. They should work, said my uncle, flying into a rage, even if they have to sweep up horse dung, it serves them right, they should learn to work.

My father's academic degree had always been a thorn in my uncle's side, as was my father's indifference over pecuniary matters. My mother was steadfast in wanting to let us continue our studies despite everything, although she wasn't ambitious and hardly thought it would lead to careers for us, but my uncle ran her down for that, said it was living beyond our means, he would have liked to see us children temporarily and, as he probably convinced himself, for educational purposes, treated like dirt, so that he could later raise us up to his level, which in my case would have meant an apprenticeship in his business.

If you should ever make public the story of *that* pair of doves, your relatives won't exactly be thrilled, says Beat with a sardonic grin.

Beat loves dining out by himself in Paris; the meals can never last long enough for him. He also loves the company of young ladies, but he prefers to keep the one separate from the other, I think he's a confirmed bachelor. I can well imagine him dropping a female acquaintance because the lady's presence while he was dining didn't please him; thanks to too much vivacity or a certain sort of absent-mindedness, talkativeness, thoughtlessness, gluttony, or anything at all that he might consider to be in bad taste, she could have made it impossible for him to partake of his meal in the manner he so loves: appreciatively and circumspectly and with a hint of ritual. On the following day, he would have to go *alone* to a clean, well-lit, high-quality three-star restaurant that suited him perfectly, and he would strictly refrain from having a cigar between the individual courses, even if the time between said courses stretched out interminably, because he, as a nonsmoker out of principle, would only allow himself a cigar with his cognac after coffee, and during the meal he would consider himself lucky to be alone and to be able to dwell on such questions of style undisturbed.

I ask myself how my dear friend Beat behaves with women, he's always making their acquaintance everywhere, even on the bus, and of course it always starts with him taking them out. I think he's a terrific listener and he knows how to give the ladies the impression that they're being fully understood, finally, for once, they feel understood and not ambushed; and they also feel protected, a discreet masculinity is directing things, even if unobtrusively, and this masculinity is combined with a high degree of cleanliness, the delicate scent of aftershave, which only reaches the lady's nostrils now and then, so that she's already forgotten this sensory impression by the time she smells it again, a subtle tangy smell, not sweet, not exotic, not reminiscent of pomade or of hair treated with pomade, it's a clean, masculine scent, and with all that, with all his discretion, the lady decides that her new acquaintance is not the least bit boring, and certainly not sexless, but rather, presumably, when they reach that stage, that he'll be a terrific lover.

You're a creature of instinct, you glow, you've an incandescent mantle, I say to him, I don't know if he likes to hear that, he doesn't reply, but afterward he smiles this special, mischievous smile that can mean all sorts of things, in some respects he's so secretive that one might suspect him of being quite depraved, behind closed doors, and, yes, he can also be brusque, because everything has its limits.

He's a confirmed bachelor *and* a notorious admirer of women, he delights in women. Discriminating, all too discriminating perhaps, he'd probably go for it if he found all the qualities that he appreciates now in different women united in a single person, if he met the perfect woman, yes, then he wouldn't hesitate a moment; but as it stands he prefers to procrastinate and drag things out. It's difficult to make a decision, and as the years go by, it gets more and more difficult. And now he says, I don't know if he says it to irritate me or out of brotherly love, as it were, to be on the safe side, nevertheless, in spite of everything, he says, you should find yourself a steady girlfriend—but he no longer mentions his cashier idea.

No, I don't want a girlfriend. I have ONE, who is always on my mind, although I can't stand to think about her. I force myself not to think about her, I do everything possible to keep myself from doing so. I tell myself: maybe it isn't a case of love poisoning, it isn't so bad at all. I tell myself: it's wonderful to be so free in such a city, where the table is always set and ready for you, by table I mean those establishments, these *maisons de rendez-vous* where I like so much to go, to Madame Julie's house, for example. I tell myself: what you find there is also something like love, and I think of Dorothée, or of Laurence, of Virginie—

But now I'm thinking of Laurence, yes, I met her at Madame Julie's, where else, but then she also received me at her home.

I'm climbing up somewhere out of the Metro, almost like a thief, no, but with pent-up anticipation, nervously; by the way, I love this special nervousness in me, it may appear as shyness, because it leaves me breathless, unable to speak, but it's just because I'm looking forward so very much to the encounter, I also toy with the thought of not going after all, of turning back at the last moment, I'm still leaving it open, but at the same time I'm worried that I might have come in vain, it's possible that I might have come on the wrong day, or that she's forgotten our arranged meeting.

Now I'm climbing up the stairs from the Metro, I'm not going to say where, I'm free and have an amorous afternoon ahead of me. This neighborhood can't be compared with my quarter, the streets are wider, the people are different, above all there's *more light*—the big city blocks are axially aligned so you can see a long way in each direction—then I come to a point where the Metro glides along aboveground, at another place I see the foreshortened tracks shooting straight into the light. I turn into the familiar side street, a street without any businesses at all, the only exception to that, I read, being a maternity home, private and probably prohibitively expensive. I go past the maternity home, I take the next street to the left at the intersection, there's a lot of greenery on this street, there are even gardens in front of the tall, very exclusive homes or residences where happy children are playing, I hear children's laughter. The air resounds with birdsong, a vague warbling of idleness, discretion is assured. The lobby of Laurence's building is huge, like in a luxury hotel, it opens out to various staircases, I search the many nameplates for hers, press the buzzer, now her voice comes through the intercom, I go to the elevator.

The door of Laurence's apartment is ajar, hello, Laurence. Then I go inside, into this high-ceilinged, spacious room that is now darkened and contains a large bed, also a glass table, cupboards, and closets in the background, on the glass table all sorts of small porcelain ornaments, glasses, decanters, on the walls tasteful pictures of butterflies, a small door leads into a pantry. Filtered afternoon light is coming in through the narrow gaps in the shutters that are rolled down outside the windows. Laurence is wearing a three-quarter-length dress that reaches far below her knees, it doesn't suit her, she smiles in her half-Vietnamese way. How are you? asks the smile and this voice, which to me seems slightly Chinese.

I still have the quiet street with the chirping birds and the children's voices in my ears, I blink in the darkened room in anticipation of the coming event, of the happiness I will experience, and at the same time it occurs to me that not a soul on earth knows where I am, not even you, Beat.

Laurence doesn't look exactly sexy in her garden-party dress, just neat and, yes, very respectable. We drink a little, while we sit beside each other almost demurely on the wide bed with its patchwork quilt, in the half-light of the darkened room. The sounds of the late afternoon come humming in through the open windows. The siren of an ambulance winds its way through the steady hum, and in the background, the surf of evening noise, the rush hour, is already slightly audible.

We sit on the bed, smoke, sip at our glasses, chat. Laurence has adopted this overly polite tone of hospitality, her voice has a nasal pitch that I attribute to her having a father from the Far East, and it gives her an expression of inscrutability, Laurence is a Eurasian.

You've already said that several times, says Beat, she's a Eurasian—and what else? For all I care she could be a Hottentot.

She wears panties and a bra that say DIOR, I reply. Would you like to have her address?

You're a racist and in addition to that you think you're a member of the master race and furthermore you're a braggart, says Beat with a face that's more than just surly, the mask of surliness is designed to hide the fact that he's also a voyeur.

I say: Beat, I say, you're just jealous because you don't have the guts to go to such establishments. You find it *vieux jeu* and bourgeois and reactionary, probably even fascist—but maybe you're just afraid of getting an infection, you hygiene freak? And besides, I don't give a damn about your advice, the last thing in the world I need is someone like that cashier of yours. To pick up a cashier and take her out with the intention of getting her into bed and keeping up with her just so she'll be on call for sex would just be too insincere for me. I would have to feign feelings I don't feel, and whenever I took her out to dinner or the movies, I'd always be thinking that I was just buying her. Whereas with Laurence there's no talk about love, that's where I go to *make* love, which doesn't exclude my having all kinds of feelings into the bargain. And I have to say that when I've *paid* to make love with a prostitute, if it's done well, everything seems pricelessly beautiful to me afterward, like a gift. Long live France and long live the former Indochina, long live this entire great culture, because so much tact and knowledge can only be explained on a cultural basis. Do you understand now why I love to abstain from all high-minded forms of culture, why I avoid the writers and artists and intellectuals, why I don't give a damn about them? Culture either proves its worth in everyday life, for example in the brothel, or it doesn't count, I say to Beat.

To myself I think: it's impossible to know about things like sexuality, let alone to speak about them. If I knew about it, then I wouldn't have to do it anymore, or at least not as often. One either talks about it or one does it. I have to do it, because I still don't understand it. Go there yourself, do it yourself, leave me alone, I imagine myself saying to Beat.

I turn the radio on.

ACCEPT ME, CREATE ME! I cried out to the city, I cried out because the city was either deaf or was giving me the cold shoulder. The city now seemed to be of an often glacial beauty, cold to the point of freezing me to death; it probably seemed like that to me because I was projecting my panic onto it, rigidity and coldness were the reflection of my own state of mind: this feeling of being a foreigner.

And yet I had often come to Paris, even as a young boy, when my aunt, who had lived here through the war, sent for us in her euphoria at having survived; later on I came again and again, for brief visits, and also to work here for short periods of time. I had always come here to recharge my batteries, to bathe in the waters. But now I had come to Paris to stay: I had given up my home in Switzerland, my wife, my relatives, my homeland, now I was sitting in this gigantic city as if caught in a trap. Paris was now my day-to-day reality, but what was I supposed to do in a stony reality of such vastness, where I myself still had no daily routine, no daily world of work that shielded me by keeping me occupied; that would have shrunk Paris down to my size.

I also couldn't take refuge anymore with this or that acquaintance, I had the sea of houses, but I didn't have a single friend, just the concierge, and because I no longer felt the urge to explore Paris, Paris no longer meant anything to me. I didn't stroll around anymore, I hid myself away, I went to a café that I called *The Sad Café*, where there was a bird, I think it was a jackdaw, that hopped around on the bar or the counter, and an English couple sat next to me at dinner, studying the street map, and somewhere in the background the owner and his relatives were watching television, and I thought of the fact that I would soon be going home again, and that absolutely nothing awaited me there but my loneliness.

I also couldn't write during these early days in Paris, I had a warped relationship to the past and felt paralyzed about the future, I no longer had access to anything I was used to, and I would soon run out of money, my fears came creeping forth like vermin from every crack and corner.

I felt unable to do even the simplest thing, to undertake anything, it was an almost physical paralysis. And my inaction began to torment me, then set off panic attacks. Suddenly my background knowledge moved into the foreground and I was faced with the reality of my insecurity, the reality of my apathy. This isn't a bad mood, it's not transient indisposition, it's your current reality, I thought, and now the fact that I had emigrated took on an entirely different appearance: what will I do, I thought, if I can't shake off this apathy, or if it becomes morbid; what if it turns out to be what psychiatrists call an *endogenous depression*? This thought bit me like a snake, sinking its teeth firmly into me, and now I was afraid that something might just shut down in my head. I remained fixated on this fear that I was still just able to suppress; and I felt the walls around me start to freeze.

What if this endogenous depression *had* already taken hold of me? First the thought occurs to me, and then, when it falls on fertile soil, that is, when it finds an unarmed, permeable state of mind, a superstitious fear arises: now the thought is circulating, the poison is circulating through my veins, now I can no longer be sure what was there first, my toying with the idea, or the symptom, now I wait spellbound for other symptoms to appear.

What if I *had* to lose contact with people, what if it were all according to plan, if this losing contact was a function, an emanation of this endogenous depression or illness that had been festering in me for quite some time; what if I had burned my bridges and emigrated because of some compulsion. And my last visits in Zürich, where nothing of consequence had been said, hadn't they been stubbornly, deliberately missed and wasted opportunities to save myself? Hadn't I simply refused to clutch at straws?

Maybe I had simply been assailed by the thought of my insecurity at my most vulnerable moment; but I kept thinking about it, what if I now, here, were to succumb entirely to this melancholy passivity. I have to pull myself together, I have to watch out, I can't let myself go to this extent, I said to myself, but by then I was having a full-fledged panic attack. Am I sick? Has melancholy always been my prevailing mood, was my old fear of boredom, my fear of emptiness, and my corresponding desire to live life to the fullest perhaps always symptomatic of it? And my ability to get enthusiastic about things, the infectious élan vital that people attributed to me, have I always had to act that way to *counteract* a lethargy and depression festering inside me? Had I basically always been in solitary confinement, in a state of dangerous interior isolation? And the women, had that possibly been an obsessive-compulsive neurosis: to escape from this deep-seated isolation; was my élan, my occasional love of life, my exuberance nothing more than a crazed rampage *against* the disease that held hidden in it the threat of death? And now all that was finally forcing its way to the surface in the trap I had set for myself, according to plan, the trap called Paris—

I was confronted by the two terribly dilapidated rooms that hadn't been tidied up in a long time, and confronted by the thought that I would be *incapable*, in a clinical sense incapable of doing anything about it. And outside, there was the city—the further wall around me, of my own choosing.

Now I'm like Florian, I thought, if not worse. And now I also saw my previous books in a new light, as having been an enormous effort, for my capabilities a well-nigh Herculean effort. They were superhuman achievements insofar as they represented desperate attempts to escape my creeping depression, if not mental derangement, this feeling that my life was running out, or could never, never ever be restored, this feeling of dying, a form of lethargy—and my books were nothing but the persistent fight against that, a self-defense, an attempt to revive myself. That's how I saw it. Against the background of this illness, my books seemed to me to be the work of Titans. How had I ever been able to pull myself together, how had I always managed to do it?

Accept me, create me, I whispered to the city when I could finally pluck up my courage and break loose, when I hastily left my box-room and ran to the nearby Metro station to get away from myself and go for a ride. I got off at Station Cité and walked along Notre-Dame to Île Saint-Louis. Everything was familiar to me, the beautiful narrow streets that followed the natural contours of the island, the bridges, the Seine, the monuments that can be seen upstream and downstream from the bridges, the wharfs, the walls along the wharfs, the trees standing against the walls, everything was there and I knew it, as my brain wanted to inform me, but now everything loomed motionless, the Seine seemed to be made of theatrical metal foil, driven along as part of a stage set accompanied by artificial sounds, the buildings like backdrops.

I wept dry tears on that walk, couldn't breathe life into anything, I was the one who had gone so numb, I was the culprit. I crept around like a thief, concerned only that no one should figure out that I'd already died, because otherwise I'd be caught and arrested. My feet walked through a glass world, then again through a lunar landscape, and I knew that nothing else awaited me now anywhere in the world.

I'll freeze to death, I'll die in this cold; and then, as I went home, I thought: I'll just let it happen. This icy city will either kill you or recreate you anew. You can't go anywhere, at most you can go further and further into it.

Where, for God's sake, should I go? I asked. *Into the forest*, said a voice. And I thought of poor Stolz, my youthful doppelgänger who had frozen to death one winter in Spessart Forest. He had always gone just *to the edge of the forest*, and the first time he went *into* the forest, he hadn't found his way out again. This young man, whose life really never got started, had gone to a lonely, unfamiliar farm in Spessart to write his thesis, thinking he would benefit from the quiet and isolation. But it didn't come to that, he got sleepier and sleepier at the farm. There was little possibility of contact with others there, and his freely chosen exile turned out to be a trap. He'd never had many interests, and here, the lethargy to which he had always been inclined broke out in him pathologically until he slept it all away. His later freezing to death, after getting lost in the woods in winter and walking until he was exhausted, was just the physical reenactment of a process to which he had long since inwardly succumbed. He had always been surrounded by this silent forest that threw him back onto his own resources, but he had gone neither into the forest nor into himself.

And now a voice had whispered to me that I too had to go *into the forest*. Into which forest? Into the forest where this lethargy dwelt. I'll write my way in, I told myself, I have to stride right into the fear. I'll make it my daily exercise to find out about it, I'll use this exercise against the city, I have no other option. I'll spin a cocoon around myself and then free myself from it.

Accept me, create me. If I overcame the fear, if I entered the forest by writing, if I clung to my writing and didn't let up, if in this way I came to myself, came back to life, then it wouldn't just be a survival, but a new life. From this test that the city set for me, I would emerge a different person. This city is a hard school, it can destroy you as well as work wonders. It will be your teacher.

And I thought of the many people who had arrived here before me with the very same hope, and whom the city had delivered from something. I thought of George Orwell, who had gone through the school of hunger here, of misery; I thought of the young Hemingway, who faced his wartime trauma while writing here, writing about his alter ego Nick Adams, who had trembled with fear at the Piave front, and on long nights had mentally fished the river for fear his soul would leave him if he fell asleep; I thought of Henry Miller, who had freed himself here from his American nightmare and from his writer's block; and how he wrote! I thought of those who were robbed of their homeland, the refugees Joseph Roth and Walter

Benjamin. Admittedly, they had taken their lives at the end, the one with absinthe, the other with poison while fleeing the Nazis—but with what contempt for fear, with what style had they dared to ignore the "city" at that time, the threat at that time.

I thought of poor Vincent van Gogh, who had arrived here as a backwoodsman who painted in somber earth tones, and in Paris he literally found his way *to the light*—to his light, to his ecstasy of color. I thought of his ability to stay the course, no, his ability to struggle through, and of his disposition, that people found hard to tolerate in Paris, this fanaticism, the mania to convert people; I thought of him, and when I first discovered the building, 56 Rue Lepic, where he had lived together with his brother Theo, I saw him before my eyes going through these very streets with a still-wet canvas under his arm, coming from Place Blanche or from Butte.

But now I thought of Sandro Thieme, the German painter I met at the end of the 1950s. He was several years older, he had been through the war, and after a short apprenticeship with Baumeister in Stuttgart he had moved directly to Paris. We met because he lived with a dancer who was my then-wife's sister, and when the two of them dropped in on us in Bern, then it seemed to me that, in comparison to them, I wasn't living a real life yet, instead, I lived and worked in a sandbox; to my eyes, they were, without putting on airs, world class, they breathed the air of freedom. Back then I regularly wrote art reviews, and in that capacity I was sometimes sent to Paris, and when I arrived at Gare de l'Est in the early morning, I took a taxi right out to Sandro's place in Montparnasse; he lived, specifically, on Rue de la Tombe-Issoire, in a little summerhouse in an inner courtyard, and he had lovingly improved it, in this little house there was not only a studio, but also a living room, even a kitchen and shower with hot and cold water—to acquire such comforts Sandro had tapped into the city mains. There was also a sleeping compartment on a second floor built into the studio, to which one could climb up, if one had a head for heights and felt courageous, on a spiral staircase with small steps; there was everything, just in miniature, the shower took up at most half a square meter of floor space, the kitchen not much more, the living room reminded me of a cabin on a boat, with the furniture interlocking as in a puzzle, it took the skill of a contortionist to wind one's way through, but once one was sitting down, the seating was solid and even comfortable.

Only the studio had the feeling of space, because it had a high ceiling, and because of its large windows it was also light, even if it was crammed full to overflowing with paintings and painting utensils, with equipment, with all the things accumulated by his having painted there for years. There was a fence around the summerhouse, and with a narrow path in between, it bordered on another fence that enclosed a somewhat more modern hut. This is where Sandro's neighbor lived with his Creole girlfriend and his dog, he was an American who had come over as a pianist, and indeed had arrived with a gigantic American car and with money, of course a grand piano too, but in the meantime, due to ever greater consumption of drugs and alcohol, he had gone to rack and ruin. He was still able to maintain his conspicuous car for a while as a status symbol, but in the end the car was nothing more than a monument, since the motor had been taken out and sold. In my time, the car no longer existed, although he apparently still had the grand piano, which he hardly ever played, and he still had the beautiful Creole, who sometimes chatted from fence to fence with Sandro's girlfriend. It looked a little like a painting by Gauguin that shows a similar-looking woman at a fence and is called *Bonjour Monsieur Gauguin*.

In the middle of the golden age of tachisme, Sandro painted figuratively, he painted pictures with an element of surrealism, for example a woman-tree, with the woman's limbs thorny, in positions ranging from monstrous to obscene. He worked on these images over a long period of time, using the techniques and patience of the old masters, and with an attitude that seemed removed and philosophical despite the potentially offensive subject matter. Later on, under the relaxing, warming influence of his partner, as he had to admit, because she insisted on it, he did still lifes that made a less thorny impression, they seemed Italian, in contrast to his earlier works, which resembled those of Hieronymus Bosch.

She addressed him as "my sunshine," or other such names; she made him more pleasant; to her, he looked like a cherub. He was a tall, sinewy fellow with wide shoulders, who could look really good, especially when he had thrown on a jacket; tall, thin, with a long head—his girlfriend liked to say it looked like a figure from an Egyptian mural. Sandro had a hard, high forehead, almost like a vertical cliff face, with very deep-set eyes under long lashes. And he looked out from under the vault of his eyebrows with a rather surly, almost nasty expression, hard and angry like someone distraught yet unable to speak. But his face could warm up, it started in his eyes and softened his cheeks and mouth, then this shy smile material- ized, he seemed to drag it all the way up to his frontal sinus cavities, so that one thought, now he's even laughing up there. He had this laugh that went up to his forehead, he drove it up into his forehead with a marabou-like nodding of his head, so he didn't have to lis- ten to it himself. His sweetheart was determined to mold him into shape according to her own ideas, she found fault with him a lot, he wasn't just her baby, but also her life's work, maybe she thought she could become his muse. When he got furious, she called him "my sunshine," "my Egyptian" right away again to calm him down. It was embarrassing for anyone else present.

Sandro's shyness also expressed itself in his way of walking. If one walked down the street with him, one got the impression that he was making his way noiselessly along the edge of an abyss. He didn't often talk about the war, but I knew he had experienced the Battle of Britain as a radio operator, and when the air force was reduced due to lack of fuel and many members of the air force had to be assigned to the infantry, he had in the end experienced and survived the Battle of

Monte Cassino. He had told me of soldiers who lay with a leg stuck up out of their foxhole, their fortification, for hours, in the hope it would be hit or ripped off and so allow them to escape from that hell via the military hospital. He also described how they had gotten rid of a particularly mean officer. This officer, who'd harassed the soldiers in every way imaginable, used to inspect the men on night-watch without any advance notice, appearing like a shadow, hoping to catch them doing something against regulations; so without further ado they had gunned him down, when they called out "who's there" they had all fired together, it couldn't be determined later whose bullet had killed him, the guy was riddled with them. Sandro had deserted from Monte Cassino, he had set himself adrift in a barrel on the ocean, then made his way through occupied Northern Italy and through Germany. He was sitting in his mother's cellar in a small town in Baden-Württemberg when the war came to an end.

To a modest extent, he was also considered an up-and-comer, there were two eminent French critics who had praised him, now and then he took their reviews out of his wallet and held them in his hand as if he were holding a psalm book. I asked myself what tied him to Paris, he didn't really leave his studio, didn't take part. I couldn't get close to Sandro, in human, social, emotional terms he was a sort of invalid, but he impressed me. In him, I saw something like a spider crouching in its web, but lying in wait not so much for victims as for proofs, proofs that would support his pessimistic take on life. He collected these, evidence contributing to his inverse faith, so to speak. He told me about an elderly married couple he'd been observing for some time from the window of an acquaintance's apartment. The way the two old people withdrew to take their afternoon tea, seeming to steel themselves as if for some ritual rite, had awakened his curiosity. What he finally discovered with his binoculars seemed to belong in his gallery of absurdities: the old people didn't sit at a table, they sat down beside the bed of a laid out, life-size, naked doll whose face and genitalia were garishly made-up, they drank their tea with the most noble airs and graces, if not directly from the body parts, then at least at the head and feet of their specimen. Sandro didn't have it easy in Paris, it's true, it seemed unlikely that he would make his way. Also, his girlfriend's admiration seemed to be on the wane, her propagandistic enthusiasm had visibly lost its vigor.

In his last years, Sandro developed a sort of strategy for success. He had started painting portraits, and it looked as if he could build up a clientele with that, mainly in Germany. He had bought himself a car and now drove on many occasions to the Stuttgart area, where prosperous clients would spend a fair bit of money on a Sandro Thieme portrait. And then he had an accident on one of these trips through France in winter. He lost control of his car on an icy curve and it crashed into a tree. The horn got stuck and sounded for a long time through the winter night, terrible, and Sandro lay, with no outward sign of an injury, dead in the snow.

Why had he come to Paris? He had certainly dreamed of making his fortune here as a painter. He held Picasso in high esteem and may have come here following in his footsteps. But Picasso was no longer in Paris, he was on Olympus; and the Paris that received Sandro was the citadel of Wols, Fautrier, Soulages, Dubuffet, Mathieu, the followers of Yves Klein; there was no movement there that could have included him, influenced him, recharged him. He had a few pals, no friends; he knew an art dealer, a gallery owner on Rue de Seine, from whom he could borrow some money if necessary. What was the city to him? He had an undying love for it, even if he didn't talk about it; he loved the asylum that it offered him, as it offered everyone, along with the absolute, occasionally alarming freedom.

He must also have loved that the city was also a sort of Tower of Babel. Yes, he had probably dedicated himself to the Tower, invisible but omnipresent; he was secretly one of the people building up this Tower whose foundations lay in the darkest obscurity of the past and whose crown faded in the indiscernibility of the future, he sat on one of the countless cornices and carved hideous faces in the stone, heard the whispering and the sounds of work, the voices from distant centuries mixed with the murmuring of prophecies and talk of what was to come; there was a humming as if from a colony of bees, as if from flocks of birds that one can't see, the rushing of rivers, the sound of dust settling, of rubble falling; and the noise of factories; mating calls and the mask of madness; horses neighing and wraiths riding, ghosts wafting past.

No, I couldn't say what kept Sandro in Paris, I didn't know; I also didn't know why I was in Paris, accept me, create me, my behavior was that of a man unhappy in love trying to talk a woman into yielding to him. I was a suitor, was repeatedly rejected, and would probably die of my presumptuous love. If I was outside, on the streets, in the pushing and shoving, the flow of this bustling life, then I could feel warm and well, I was right in the midst of it, "in the city," united with it, myself an element of it, admittedly drowning in everything it had to offer, but nevertheless a part of it, sharing in it.

But if I was back in the apartment again, at my place, then I'd fallen out of it, because this being touched on all sides, because this being picked up and being part of it couldn't be simulated. Only in the fleeting union did I belong to it and feel saved by a sort of love, saved from my fate, from isolation. Saved from the agony of being without insight.

I found myself in this boxroom of a tiny apartment located on Rue Simart in the 18th arrondissement, but where was that? Where in the city, where in the world? I knew it less and less. Me in Paris? Me in Paris, France, Europe, the world, the universe?

Here I was the disappearing one, the louse, the atom, and this Here could wipe me out wherever I went; it could cast me out into the darkness, where I'd be lost, where I was helpless, a darkness that couldn't be brightened by any knowledge of the place, by any "insight." When I rode around in the evening on a well-lit bus, in this close contact with the many people now returning home from their workplaces; in the midst of these people tired after a day's work, in these smells of clothing and bodies, between people reading the newspaper, women weighed down by shopping bags full to overflowing, and among them perhaps a pretty one, a saucy one; once there was a tremendously attractive dark-skinned woman in a skirt that was tight around her knees and a jacket that emphasized her shoulders, and her hair, combed back on one side, let me see one of her temples, and her eyes, like dark gemstones afloat in their alabaster-white settings, looked shyly away from the slightest contact with a stranger's gaze and didn't look back, and on her extremely finely formed ears, heavy pendants hung from silver attachments, pulling her earlobes down and jingling gently at the slightest turn of her head; she sat lost in thought, as if behind glass, in the packed bus, and when she stood up and disappeared, a fat woman sat down with a thud on the seat that had become free, a gray person, continually grabbing at her shopping bag that kept slipping down over her short legs; and through the noise of the motor inside the bus, through the soporific sounds of the vehicle in motion, that created their own type of silence, I heard the insistent talk of what I assumed were a few black men, it was a carefree, good-natured palaver (or at least that's what it sounded like), in that unmistakable, guttural register, which could suddenly crack and switch over into a high, birdlike screeching, as if he'd suddenly lost his voice; on the bench across from me were Arabs, their faces prickly with stubble, their expressions gloomy, forever grim; when I rode along the familiar route across the city, dozing in the bus, and now and then pressing my face to the window to make out a street name, the name of a bus stop, *Vauvenargues*, *Pont Cardinet*, names that glided past, and I kept an eye out for a reference point with which I could associate the name, there, *la Clé au juste Prix*, in lettering as long as a giraffe's neck, on a tiny steel door painted ice-blue, I had wanted to take a closer look at it for a long time, I thought, but nonetheless had never gotten off the bus because I was too lethargic, but now that I had the image of this part of the street before my eyes, and how the street looked in the morning, I remembered that at exactly this place on this insignificant street something had excited or enthralled me, there was something in the air there for me, I thought, you'll have to take a closer look at this part of town, but by then we had already crossed Avenue de Saint-Ouen, then Avenue de Clichy, and now, before my inner eye, I could already see Place de Clichy with its Café Wepler, which Miller wrote about, I knew this part of town very well, it was about a forty-five minute walk from my apartment, formerly I had often taken a stroll to Clichy, down Rue Caulaincourt and past Montmartre Cemetery, whose gloomy mausoleums could be seen to the right and left from the overpass, to the right and left a city of the dead; I pushed Clichy away from me, along with its many oyster crates in front of the restaurants and the usually chaotic traffic around the monument, as I rode along, I was now observing two bearded Jews who were hanging on to two handholds near the door and swinging like jumping jacks while they had an animated conversation, they always wear these narrow-brimmed dark hats, always have beards, and always wear these black, severely tailored coats that look like kaftans, I thought, and at the same time they have some quite normal profession, but always in this—religious?—traditional costume! it's like leading a double life; and I observed their unusually lively, somehow inspired facial expressions, their conversation went on without a break as they swung back and forth, what were they talking about, now and then they laughed as if at a good joke; and I thought, now I'm riding along this stretch for the umpteenth time, I'm feasting my eyes on the same familiar sights, but I couldn't possibly claim to know the area, at the very most I recognize it very superficially, LA CLÉ AU JUSTE PRIX, and everyone riding along in the same bus would get a completely different impression of the same part of the street, the same street, as many different images as pairs of eyes, now I saw the street as something unfathomable before me, as a Darkest Africa worthy of Livingstone & Stanley, impenetrable, and from this impenetrability all these eyes took different things into account, so long as there was light enough to see, and I saw the hollows and rifts broken into small pieces by all these beams of light, into light and shadow, the street was cut up into snippets of sound too, but for everyone it still bore the same name, Rue Guy Môquet, for example, who had he been, a name rubs off on a street, Rue Guy Môquet (also written Môcquet), in the eyes of the two Jews, in the eyes of the woman whose shopping bags kept slipping down, in the eyes of the brooding Arab; I thought of the bit in Hemingway's "The Snows of Kilimanjaro" where the American writer suffering from gangrene, awaiting death, thinks of everything he hasn't gotten around to writing, he had always postponed the best things, now he would never write them; and among these precious things or subjects he had always meant to get around to describing, the thing at the top of his list was something banal: to my astonishment, to my shock, he spoke of the gurgling of the gutter and of the smells in the air and of the sounds at Place de la Contrescarpe, just as they had remained in the memory of his hero, and in his own memory, from the time when he had started to write next door on Rue Descartes, near the Panthéon; the first editions of his feelings at that time! yes, I thought, as I was riding along on the bus, he never got around to it, at least not on paper and on purpose, at most in a dream; since it can rise up again in a dream, we do have it in us, down to the smallest detail, we retain everything with heightened perception, but we never touch it again, unless in our sleep, I thought; and now I thought of Place Contrescarpe, I made the inner leap from the scene of my bus ride over to the region of the Panthéon; the thin, rational air around about this temple of dry thoughts and hard reason, a much drier, cleaner air than here, where everything smells and sweats and chatters; and right behind it the nice, messy little round park with tramps under the trees, and students and lovers sitting outside the cafés, it basically resembles the square of a small town in the country; and right nearby is the building where Verlaine died, where Hemingway wrote; from the Panthéon it's just

a stone's throw to Jardin de Luxembourg, to the many people of leisure in the multicolored shade cast by the magnificently trimmed
trees on the brown sandy soil, people taking a stroll under this canopy of trees, and people reading, thinking, talking on these ancient,
charming, wrought-iron chairs, garden chairs set out for everyone;
the cherubs and small statues of the gods playing hide-and-seek in
the foliage, a merry-go-round with a white elephant circling around,
as in Rilke's poem, "und dann und wann ein weißer Elefant," foun-
tains, highbrow; "Ami, si tu tombes, un ami sort de l'ombre à ta
place," the song of the French Resistance, is written on a monument;
down from "Boul Mich" and over the bridge onto Île Saint-Louis,
the country palace impression of the houses along Quay Bourbon,
massive paved inner courtyards with trees, and among the trees, statues, bronze statues larger than life, the heavy wooden door set in the
front gate, and outside, the quay wall, I run my hand along the wall
as I stroll past, the pavement is narrow here, a small sidewalk, I lean
over the wall, down below by the water is the path along the shore for
dogs, couples, fishers, yes, and tramps; recently I saw one lying on a
bench, in ragged clothes, he was sleeping, and the urine ran through
his pants, forming a stringy rivulet below the bench and running
down to the Seine; which I greet from Pont Alexandre when I come
from Esplanade des Invalides, on one side of the river the houses
seem to be hanging down from the sky on threads, silhouettes light
as air; but the flowing water from the bridge, there's nothing nicer
than peeing into a river from a bridge, a real feeling of elation; and
now a pleasure boat comes along, Bâteau Mouche, and all the tourists' enraptured faces gaping out through the protective glass with
their mouths open, fish faces; and the poor man peeing on the bench
who sees nothing, he's asleep;

and on to Hôtel de Ville, the evening crowd on Rue de Rivoli, it's
dirty here, the real bazaar; bazaar, I think, right: across from Bazar
de l'Hôtel de Ville, in the midst of the crowd, a young woman is
running away, holding a child by the hand, running away from two

men, she screams that they should leave her alone, shit, "laissez-moi donc, merde," she screams, the men try to cut her off, block her way, grab at her; this is getting other people's attention, they turn around, what's going on here? Kidnapping, a crime, and right here in the midst of the evening crowd; the child that's being dragged along, the innocent kid, you can't just stand by and watch that, already a group of people from the crowd is wedged in between, the pursuers are getting embarrassed, one of them takes a transmitter out of his pocket, police? what? a detective? now people hear the word shoplifting, the woman has stolen something, a pair of gloves; she keeps on screaming to let her go, "lachez-moi," the people get involved, almost all are on the woman's side, having put the pursuers in the wrong, which makes them unsure of themselves, but they tug at the woman again, the child whimpers, now it bursts into tears, poor little mite, the crowd gets furious; now the woman escapes, her pursuers want to follow her, but the crowd blocks their way, let her go, you pigs, what's the big deal, let her go, you mean bastards; the two give up, they also say "merde" and shrug their shoulders; the woman has run down the stairs to the Metro with the child and disappeared, escaped; the crowd continues discussing the incident, a well-dressed woman says, that's not right, where would we be if everyone stole things; oh, shut your trap, says a coarse woman, it's none of your business anyway; stupid cow, screams the upright woman; misery, says the other; the people disperse; that's enough of that, I say to myself, that's enough now; stop thinking about the city, you'll never get it all together, you can't think it, the city, every time you try it, you just chalk up another defeat, you can never HAVE it; you'll never have it, I thought and pressed my nose to the window, where were we?

we were just riding past a little bar, a bar like a thousand others, there's the round or long counter under neon light, in such a bar there's always the feeling that one's in a large arena, it's always as colorful as a circus, I don't know what creates that effect, maybe it's because the weak red light in the tubes, at the lower end of the color spectrum, evokes the circus when reflected by the cream-colored walls; and at the bar the few men and women drinking beer, a small white wine, a *ballon de rouge*, a *calva*, before they go home, they stretch it out, have another, quickly; they stand under the lights at the bar as if under a halo, with the glockenspiel of bottles in the background, stand on the tiled floor with the cigarette butts and bread crumbs, stand devoutly in the light, in the prayer room, as if this were their only refuge, and now the bar is simply everything: café, pub, barbershop, drugstore, emergency ward, interrogation room, waiting room, field hospital, and chapel, CONSOLATION; all in one, the best shelter on earth, one more, one more *ballon de rouge;* they stand there as if enlightened, the miracle gets around;

as we drove along, I felt the narrowing and widening of the streets, like breathing out and breathing in, I felt it in my chest; and the streets merged with all the breads and cakes in the display cases, with turnips, lettuce, halved oxen and pigs, and bars, many bars, the street a child scurried across, a child sent quickly across the street to buy a loaf of bread, a bottle of wine;

that's enough of that, I say to myself in the bus, turn it off; but I couldn't turn *it* off, there was still something there inside me that didn't want to settle down, that wasn't satisfied, I thought, I should get off this bus that keeps riding on and on, ever farther through the darkness, I should get off and go ashore in one of these illuminated bars, stand at the trough or the counter, knock back a glass, or better, several glasses at once, otherwise you're going to go crazy, I thought, but I knew I wasn't crazy at all, just wide awake; and now this dream came to mind that I had dreamed several times of late; the dream was about a sentencing, a judgment; it was right before my final high school exams that would qualify me for university, and it became clear to me that I was never going to pass the math exam, I wouldn't be able to demonstrate the requisite comprehension and thus the necessary ability for the required calculations with numbers, for solving equations, for the algebra, I couldn't think straight, that much was utterly clear to me, and what that meant was that I would never get out of high school; I was doomed to fail, and so our ways parted then before we reached the gate, all my friends passed through the gate and went out into life, I too went out into life, but on a different, solitary path, I knew that for me one entrance would remain blocked forever; now, I said to myself in the dream and in view of my former friends disappearing into the distance, now I will be excluded from all of that and from them, but I won't stay in school, I'll run away without this special requisite know-how and go out into life; of course I'll always be marked with this blemish, a sort of pariah, I'll always be missing *one* key, but that doesn't have to mean that I won't find my way anywhere; this dream had astonished me, because in reality I did indeed pass my final high-school exams, even if I'd only just scraped through the math, I had slipped through and had even completed a university degree, all without particularly applying myself; but in the dream I hadn't made it, in the dream I had the feeling, and the feeling had the authoritativeness of a death sentence, that I would be marked with this blemish like a curse or an illness for the rest of my life, and that I had to make up for this deficiency through a supreme effort in another field; in the dream, I hadn't been at all without hope, just a little melancholy; but why was I dreaming here and now—at my age!—about having failed this exam? did it have to do with my feeling lost in the city, this obtuse-ness and melancholy resulting from that feeling, I wondered on the bus, if not the acute danger of an endogenous depression? might I have been able to approach the city differently through "mathemat-ics," might I indeed have been able to *arrive*? surely it couldn't be a matter of rational understanding, or was that the case after all? would it have helped me if I'd been able to understand, to see *through* the city in its historical layers? if by virtue of the intellectual ability to reconstruct it the *Gestalt* of the city would have become not only understandable, but also transparent to me? would the city's thou-sands upon thousands of faces then disappear, these faces that yield only darkness? could I in such a case put on the city like a cloak (if only, that is, I possessed this other key)? but, as it is, I'll always have to piece it together, I told myself; is there a reading (of reality), a way of measuring it without losing the present, that unfathomable, puzzling aspect which, however, is essential to life: does such a complex answer exist, an answer that signifies both restoration in the sense of repair *and* an indestructible present?

you, I told myself, have always been afraid of destruction, of the destruction of the puzzle, or of life, when you try to think and analyze; you prefer the atmospheric approach through touch and smell, through conjuring things up; and what you create is ultimately this eternal fog you can never see through; you aren't looking for clarity; are you afraid of disillusionment? you never seek the "truth," whatever that may be, you seek the darkness, the darkness of your mother's womb;

you correspond like a one-man telegraph office with the *outside* of the phenomenon, but in the end you fall back into the blackest black of the inside, because you can't decode the incoming messages, can't even count them, let alone process them; both your sender and receiver are constantly in turmoil, but you remain speechless;

nevertheless, it frequently seems as if I have the word, the secret, on the tip of my tongue, I interjected; I'm often close to it;

close to what, damn it?

to a street, for example, so close to it; a Parisian street, magnificently drifting, which contains everything; I stand trembling with excitement in the middle of the street, and in its sugary, chalky facades, and in the sky between them, that patch of sky invented by this street, because the street engulfs it, the street gazes adoringly at me; I myself am the street, I am its carrier and wing; I am the fluttering of its flanks, the blinking of its Venetian blinds, the slate and sheet-metal hat on its roofs, the blushing of its skin, the grilles that veil its windows, I am the wrinkles, all the wounds and runes, I am all the darkening and brightening of its expressions, its countenance, that's me, even if I don't understand it; I am it and feel it;

the breathing of the sidewalk at its feet; all the debris under the awnings, every single reflecting glass store window and what's behind it, everything—

I hang like a puppet from the thousands of strings, eye strings, mind strings, feeling and thought strings, connected to the street by these strings, its walls and cracks slip me its messages; I hang and wriggle on the strings that make me jerk, I'm a jumping jack; it pulls on me until I collapse, fall into the gutter, a lifeless thing that the sewage washes away; that's the destruction, the darkening in the middle of the day, the darkening in the city; because I can't say it; I feel it, but don't understand; I can't grasp it—

and now I thought, while riding the bus: maybe it was this shutting of doors, this *turning away*, that drove me to women, wanting to be looked after; and now it occurred to me how in that summer, it was the hottest summer anyone could remember, a heat that brought us all down to the same level, glowing dryness with grass fires and forest fires, whole countries desperate for rain, a crooked street ran down from Rue des Abbesses in the direction of Boulevard Rochechouart, and down below there I saw a huge black whore sitting on the fender of a car; I was amazed that she could stand it, I thought to myself that her rear end must have been quite scorched already, I approached her and then followed her up an unspeakably stinking staircase into a bug-ridden partitioned room, it was stiflingly hot inside, this is where you're going to catch the infection, I said to myself, as I stood there and watched her undress, she did so in the laziest manner imaginable, maybe because she was so tall—and it was so hot, and in that very moment my nose detected the roasting smell from a frying pan or the smell of hot fat, and with that smell I was suddenly back in my childhood, it was a mother's smell, and I threw myself on the giantess, who called out something to me in her language, maybe she said, take it easy, man, not so rough, think of the thermometer! and then I walked back down the rickety stairs and loved the street and this city ardently, just as if I had been accepted, included, in any case, I belonged to it;

and now my line of thought went back to that earlier time, when I had come here to visit Sandro Thieme in his summerhouse on Rue de la Tombe-Issoire; I had spent the day with him and had visited my aunt in the evening on Rue Condorcet below Pigalle, it had gotten very late, I was on my way home, walking along deserted and empty streets where everyone was already asleep, and then I heard an electrifying sound ahead of me, the clicking of high heels, the high heels staccato, I ran through the night, following the sound, and then, a shout ahead of me, I saw a swaying white satin dress in the blackness of the night, land! I've sighted land! I rejoiced, it was a black-skinned woman from Martinique, we climbed up the stairs of a hotel together, I took hold of her as we went up, and she rubbed her bottom against me good-naturedly, and for a long time afterward, all the next day, which I spent at Sandro's, I could still smell her body, I held on to the smell and smiled at it in thought;

I never could collect the city in me, whenever I tried to, it withdrew in the sparkling sea of a bursting fireworks display and was immediately extinguished, I could only ever participate in a small corner, a street corner, wherever I happened to find myself, I could never get into this city; you can never break in through the armored skin that so-called reality holds in front of you, at least not with any composure, so would I always remain outside? while I was right in the middle of it, would I remain outside?

that's enough of that, I thought in the bus, and now I was pleasantly tired from the ride; but riding, I thought, I like to do that for its own sake; even more than riding the bus, I like riding the Metro, because then I'm "inside" the city, in its bowels; I'm among the many who smell of rain, of moisture, of skin, of their district, of work or of leisure, of perfume, of poverty, of education, of danger, of wear and tear, of a dream or of fear, of meekness, of this city where they will have their day and pass away, and within each of them is a fragmentary perception of the city, but taken all together those perceptions would yield the sum that no one has yet been able to comprehend, life isn't long enough for that; but in the rat runs of the Metro, in the bowels of the city, we are all in it, even if only in its excrement, mixed in with it;

and then out of this submissive, dirty "having," out of Hades, rolling up an escalator into daylight; one time in the Metro I saw only mouths, across from me the pursed lips of a black man; and women's lips, all these embryos emerging—until I had to look away; and riding again through the long, round, tiled tunnels, their lighting casting this zebra pattern, this illusion of a ribbed vault on the ceiling, the notes of invisible musicians wandering through the corridors; and then the few stretches where the subway escapes the gullet and becomes an elevated railroad; suddenly the car is flooded by daylight, now I'm sitting as if in a circus ride and can see a street like this from above through the cast-iron struts of the overhead railway structure: the deep ravine into endless horror, the ravine that contains all colors, I say to myself: everything is there in the light, and as the long straight streets catch the light, everything is there, the sides with their hint of black from the ironwork below the windows and balconies, the pavement below shimmering with the luster of a baker's oven, the low hat or helmet roofs, there! and the fire wall decorated with a huge advertisement that is flaking off and faded, and the high, narrow front of a corner house, the narrow cliff, on which the veins separate in the pointed corner; and the café under the awning and the few tables and chairs in front of it; the tree that mediates between its heavy trunk and its spiritual branches, not to forget the slapping flags of its leaves; and the parking car and the scream fading away and the body of someone who has just been stabbed to death and is dying by the curbside, a cadaver; and the couple having sex pressed against the wall; the whole-grain bread being taken across the street;

and then again the craziest crowd of people, as dense and teeming and noisy as a colony of penguins, it's the crush around the department store TATI at Barbès-Rochechouart; and back again into the gullet, into the entrails, into the dark;

I'd like to ride on like this forever on my railway through the mountains and valleys, in order to remain in this HAVING, to have without possessing, *I can't express what you are, but I can traverse you*;

you're not looking for clarity at all, I now hear the voice of my dear friend Beat, everything you're looking for is this feeling of Being Rocked in Darkness, you're looking for darkness, little one, says Beat;

you're right, I say, that's exactly it: I'm looking for the darkening oblivion that gives birth to memory; until in the middle of the day, in the middle of Paris, I can say: I remember, hello!

When I was younger, I was always afraid of nightfall, for years, really, until quite recently, all told, I was still terribly afraid of the night. It was mainly the feeling of being cut off when the daylight disappeared, when nothing more would arrive, nothing more come to entertain me. It was like a power failure, everything stopped, no more listeners, no more speakers. Who am I? where do I belong? where should I want to be, hope to be? I no longer knew.

The last time I experienced that feeling was in Serrazzano, a little place along the cliffs in the province of Pisa, where I had withdrawn to a vacant house belonging to some friends, almost ten years ago. I sat in this glassed-in veranda, by day it had a view of all the Tuscany Hills, and in good weather I could see as far as the ocean. I sat under the whitewashed beams that ran diagonally across the sloping ceiling; the floor was made of clay tiles in a pleasantly pale terracotta. When I pressed my nose to the window at night, I saw the stars and the crescent moon, otherwise blackness. I was sitting in a glass cockpit in the black night sky; in a very well furnished room: at the window there was a low sofa bed under a beautiful old ottoman quilt, close to the fireplace a group of armchairs and a table in the Bauhaus style, curved, springy steel and black varnished wood, all in a slightly decrepit state. It was a wonderful room, especially for working in, but first I had to fight against my fear of the night, which I thought I had long since overcome.

So when I was first there I frequently drove to the neighboring villages to escape my feeling of being a prisoner, I drove, for example, to Larderello, a ten-kilometer drive along a winding road. There, the inn LA PERLA awaited me, a barracks-like wing of a building with a restaurant. Behind the illuminated door was the large, sparsely furnished bar area with an extra-long counter and several small tables. The first time I went there, I had chatted with an eighty-year-old, a regular, and in doing so, as if under some compulsion—why, actually?—my Italian had become much more broken than necessary, so our conversation took place in that emphatic diction that locals all over the world reserve for foreigners. There is an emphasis in the intonation as if every word is being spelled out, letter by letter, for the sake of making oneself understood. I found out that the man was eighty, got up every morning at six to take care of his hens and rabbits, had been drinking wine and smoking as long as he could remember, was never bored, always had something to do, and always came to LA PERLA in the evenings for a chat. I found out that his son had just retired. I found out that the old man had a television, that he regularly went to bed around eleven, that he wore a Swiss watch and was satisfied with it. We also spoke about the relationship between the lira and the franc. Outside, it stank of sulfur; there was a sulfur spring there, indeed a sulfur bath. Men came into the cold room out of the blackness of the night, they went to the bar to drink an *aperitivo*. At eight, not a moment earlier, there was something to eat. The young man at the bar put on a white waiter's smock and led the gentlemen into the adjoining dining room. Then the owner came in too, with a sullen expression, he came from his private quarters with the look of someone who'd just gotten out of bed; later the cook also put in an appearance, a hugely fat woman, she wore a sort of nun's habit, and she had what the owner was lacking, the ability to carry on a conversation, indeed endlessly. After the meal, the few guests went over into the adjacent room where there was a television. Once it showed an old French film about a penal colony, with Gérard Philipe. I had admired him as a schoolboy in *Le Diable au corps* (with Micheline Presle), it was a film that affected me very deeply at the time. After La Perla I drove home through the quiet countryside in the night. In my cockpit I turned the radio on right away.

When I didn't go to Lardarello, I could drive to Castagneto, or to Volterra, but both of those were longer trips, to which I seldom treated myself. In Volterra, in the vicinity of the cathedral, the door of a coach house was slightly ajar, revealing the front end of an elegant old Lancia, and only when I peeked inside did I see the grandiose black and silver cargo bed built to accommodate a coffin. Later, men cloaked and cowled in black came along, carrying funeral-procession staffs in their hands. And hardly was I back in Serrazzano than I scented the atmosphere of death there too. I felt it in the way people were standing together outside the entrance to a house, there was something in the air that gave one pause, something composed of fright and pain and curiosity. Later the villagers joined the procession. As I found out, it was for an old man who had committed suicide. People said he hadn't gotten over the loss of his wife and had jumped out the window. He had lain there, just a little blood coming out his nose, but otherwise without visible injury. When his daughter arrived from Siena, people had kept quiet about the circumstances of his death, she was an unstable person. They pretended it had been a heart attack.

I sat in my glass cockpit when the storms came, leaving me in the dark even during the day, I sat for days in a sea of mist, contending with the sounds of the storm in addition to the darkness, so I listened to the radio, to the announcer's conversational voice, to the ads, the music. When the fog lifted, as the storms abated, I drove to

Castagneto Carducci. The one, main bar, the central meeting place of the small town, was already surrounded in the early afternoon by the local personalities. Since there wasn't much going on, they reacted to even the slightest hint of something happening as though it were part of some sinister conspiracy. Each of them played his assigned role on the stage of their small town. There was the somewhat corpulent, well-dressed, middle-aged man, an educated person, who emphatically greeted a gaunt nobleman, as if they hadn't seen each other from time immemorial. And the village idiot went past, toeing in, a little stooped. His hair shorn short, his skull bare, and his eyes rather squinty, though these contained, at the same time, something of a cunning sparkle.

Next to the Rosticceria, there was a very sophisticated old lady standing in front of a fruit stand, unable to make up her mind what to buy. The fruit smelled good, and the reddish buildings rose up like cliffs at the edge of the small town, and somewhere washing was fluttering in the fresh wind that came from the sea. There was a slapping sound like flags, like sails, the ocean sky tugged at the small town, as if it wanted to pull it away from its anchor and get it sailing, as if it wanted to engulf it. Something ripped off and broke away, and immediately there was a sense of departure in the air, and those left behind grew smaller and smaller, became indistinguishable, in the eyes of someone who was saying good-bye, as he drew farther and farther away.

The old lady at the fruit stand was being difficult, indeed finding fault, she expressed various concerns, she had recently heard or read about cholera outbreaks. The matron behind the stand assured her that all her fruit was perfectly fresh, but the old lady remained obstinate. Then she paid an outstanding bill and sniffed around a while longer. And the change, is it for me? asks the matron. Not on your life! says the old lady, picks it up, dumps it into her purse, and walks off.

The fear of nightfall, which I last felt in my friends' house in

Tuscany, didn't bother me for a long time, but when I first moved to Paris, I developed this fear that my life was coming to an end, that my soul would stop breathing in and breathing out. I hadn't yet properly arrived in my new life, or I didn't have the courage to have arrived, on account of my wife. For a while we still spoke on the phone, but my wife's voice always sounded like a reproach, and she didn't bother to conceal her resentment, although I knew she had, in the meantime, rebounded and entered into an entirely new life of her own. I should have been relieved about that, and I was, but at the same time I held it against her that she had broken new ground so soon, as if *she* had taken something away from me, or as if the decisiveness of her new direction would retroactively prove our common history false. We refrained from calling from then on. Soon we would also be legally divorced.

I was despondent, I was wriggling in the net of all sorts of anxieties, even hypochondria, I saw the awkwardness of my existence, I also saw the luxury of my situation, above all in comparison to the countless poorer people around me, but none of that helped, I was freezing. Sometimes I saw myself as someone already well on the way to being institutionalized, or as one of these figures who draw attention to himself on the street, because something, one doesn't know what, isn't quite right about him; there's something, an indication of nobility, or even just a flowing mane, that doesn't fit in with the poverty and especially the fear expressed by the rest of the person's appearance, and it wouldn't be surprising if someone pointed to the gentleman and remarked, that's him, *him* over there, do you see him? he's the one who once . . . do you remember now? that's him . . . A has-been.

I got a foretaste of that at the beginning of a course of treatment at a health resort in Abano Terme. My doctor had wanted to send me to a mud-bath spa on many occasions because of sporadically occurring problems with a slipped disc. And since my health insurance, which was about to run out, would still pay for such a treatment, it was high time, and I took advantage of it.

In order to sort out the matter with the insurance company, I first had to travel to Zürich. I spent the afternoon and evening before my departure in my wife's apartment, she was out of the country, I still had the key, and I rashly decided I would stay there, of all places. I lay on the bed in my clothes with the drapes pulled, they were beautiful white drapes that reduced the light in an almost clinically considerate manner, the effect was created by the material, a sort of satin weave, and the drapes fell to the floor from old-fashioned brass rods with round knobs on the ends. As I lay on the wide bed in this subdued daylight and stared at the furniture, I felt more out of place than in a hotel. I had no business there anymore, I had broken in, I couldn't sleep, just pass the time, and as I did so, I saw myself as an unauthorized intruder, a squatter. I dozed until about midnight, then I drove off. I drove in my old car in the direction of the San Bernardino Tunnel and after that across the plain of the Po River into Veneto, arriving late at Abano and my hotel. The next day I got my first fango pack. I was awakened by telephone before daybreak, that was part of the routine—they start in the night and work through until about noon; they? well, the male nurses who work in this sub-kingdom reminiscent of a laundry, because of course these hotels are all erected over thermal springs. The phone call prompted me to put on the hooded bathrobe made of thick toweling provided by the hotel and ride the elevator down into this underworld, the elevator smelled nauseatingly of the acidic earth. Downstairs, first they packed me in the scalding-hot clay, then laid white towels on top of me, it's a form of being buried alive and of course comes complete with shortness of breath and fear of suffocation. I remained in that burning, then sudorific sarcophagus for twenty minutes or more, after which the worn-out male nurse came running to free me, the person commended to his care, from the terracotta coffin that had in the meantime become almost as solid as a baking pan; then the cleaning, and after that the thermal bath; the bubbling hot water, sparkling mineral water has a noticeably exhausting effect. After that I got a massage, and then, weak in the knees, I took the elevator back to my room and fell into bed.

People say the cure makes the patient listless and soft like putty at first, inside and out; I hadn't expected that, I immediately sank into a deep despondency.

That's quite normal, people told me. Herr Saurer said, people get emotional down here. At age seventy-eight, he was taking the cure for the thirteenth time. But there was also a corresponding after-effect, later on, you leave as if born anew, the ancient Romans had known that too, those inveterate gourmands; they didn't come to Abano for nothing, said Herr Saurer, a fellow countryman from Bern whom I knew from my time at the museum, from the days of my youth, for in those days, when I was serving as an assistant, he'd held an important cultural office, a high-up senior position, and in the military he'd held the rank of colonel. I hadn't seen him again in the intervening decades, now we had met up here as fango brothers and lifetime reservists as though on a weekend training exercise. The Romans, he said, had sought out Abano because of its Fountain of Youth effect, without Abano they couldn't have begun to cope with their wild way of life. Herr Saurer sat at the table next to mine in the hotel dining room.

It was an ugly but happy dining room. At those meals, I always had a Genoese man in my line of vision, in the context of Abano he was still a young man, about fifty, a dark-haired fellow with very hairy arms and darkly glowing eyes behind glasses, shyly glowing eyes. Do they look malicious or menacing, or what's wrong with the man? I asked myself at my table for one, where the bottle of wine had a little chain around its neck with a sort of license plate on it, the plate bore my room number; I always looked at the Genoese, he couldn't be overlooked, because he always came in late, when the first course had already been served. He carried his head to one side, tucked against his shoulder, which made him seem rather affected.

When he had finally seated himself, he looked around with those glowing eyes, taking in everything, myself included. He reminded me of someone, and I kept wondering who it was, until I came to the conclusion that he reminded me of the old Latin teacher in the building with the hunchbacked Fräulein Murz and poor Florian, the teacher who had always splashed water around in my bathroom, the two of them had the same pasty complexion and the same five o'clock shadow, they had at least that in common, and something in their expression as well.

The other people I saw from my table were three Austrian grand-mothers who always came marching in, a unified front, with their angular hips and short, rounded arms that seemed to have been added to their bodies as afterthoughts, and which they placed on the table after they had taken their seats. It was obvious that there was something like a hierarchy among them, a hierarchy that might have been determined by minimal differences in social standing, and in addition all three of them seemed to be teetotalers, or their leader had given an order to that effect, in any case, during the entire length of their stay, they always chose fruit juice with their hors d'oeuvres, carefully making it last by diluting it with water so that they'd have it to the end of the meal, absolving them from ordering any drinks. One of them seemed a tiny bit more luxurious than the other two, but she was also the one who tended most to comply with their leader, and that one in turn distinguished herself by a humorous curtness, both in dealing with the waiter, she gave the orders, and in deciding when the three of them would march out at her command.

I had these two tables before my eyes, but was soon familiar with many of the other guests as well, including Germans, Italians, Cana-dians, Swiss, French, Belgians, and most of them looked very rich; almost all were old or ancient and thus quite frail. They were people who had most of their lives behind them, one might be tempted to describe them as a moribund company. It occurred to me that "outside" no one took any notice of them, or simply ignored them, but here in the hotel, and twice a day in the dining room, I was forced not just to see them, but to look at them continuously, now I too belonged on this ghost train, and it soon seemed to me as if no other group of people existed at all, as if *this* was the quintessential society.

They sat like flies on the wicker chairs in front of the hotel, or in the hallway, waiting for the meal, or they sat outside on the patio of a café in the small town, silently waiting there, hundreds of them sitting around, Abano must have a hundred such hotels, all with a fango underworld, baths, and spas. And at mealtimes, the same people came into all these hotels, pattering, creeping, hobbling, crawling along, most of them seemed rich, if not filthy rich, they were very carefully dressed for dinner in formal, ceremonial wear, an evening gown, tuxedo, and dark trousers, for lunch in elegant sportswear, with different outfits from time to time, these elderly people seemed to change their clothes at every opportunity.

I couldn't see what good it did them to go to all that effort, but then I said to myself: they probably don't see themselves as they are, they see themselves differently; and now I began to ask myself if I too was the victim of a similar delusion. Was I perhaps, in my own way, just like they were, except that I saw myself differently?

The worst were the still somewhat presentable women who acted as if they were on a pleasure yacht on the Mediterranean Sea.

Twice a week, there was a ball, and then all these visitors to the spa, these people who were essentially finished, danced with each other, and, along with them, etched in their faces, horrors of the most diverse origins. For the ladies who were still a little younger, young men had been specially brought in who could really dance and looked really good, they acted as if they found their female partners particularly attractive, they courted them. During those activities I always got the feeling that everyone felt the same way I did, that everyone saw through everyone else. What had happened to my sense of self-esteem, to the way I used to see myself? it seemed to me as if I were now facing up to the fact of some incurable illness or an even worse sort of damnation. I was distraught in this Fountain of Youth milieu; I explained to a married Italian couple, both of them physicians, who had invited me to go for a walk with them into the hills and to a rustic, out-of-the-way trattoria, that I found myself in a state of mind not unlike a victim of brainwashing, as if my personality had been entirely rewritten, and if things went on this way, I'd have to get admitted to a psychiatric clinic as soon as I got out of the spa. The couple laughed as if I'd just told them a good joke about foreigners.

I remained unsure of myself, outwardly apathetic. Since I nevertheless kept an eye on the other hotel guests with apprehensive curiosity, mainly observing the divergence between their miserable appearances and the way they *wanted* to look, in other words, the phenomenon of self-deception, and in doing so detected nothing but tragicomic absurdity, it seemed a natural conclusion that I was also doing a good job of fooling myself. Had I, without knowing it, become a ridiculous figure? Was I one of those "has-beens" that one instinctively spots in a crowd?

And now I tried desperately to make contact with the self-image I'd still been carrying around with me just before being "admitted" here, that I'd still possessed a short while ago, and had even shown off, parading around with complete confidence in myself. I thought my way back to those experiences I'd had that were possibly the most "full of life," most worldly, for example to Madame Julie's *maison de rendez-vous*, to Dorothée and other purely physical relationships, I did it to arm myself against these attacks of tabula rasa. I tried to think of people who, in my youth, had been the same age I was now, and in general I began to think of people among my friends and acquaintances who were my age and older, in order to be able to assess if they were on the bright side or the dark side, did they know what life is all about or were they deceiving themselves. Should that artist, that academic, that alcoholic, that energetic businessman from my age group already be relegated to the debit side of the ledger, or should I still enter him on the side of the living? I collected counter-arguments. A Prime Minister Trudeau, I called out inwardly, no, he certainly doesn't belong here yet; I developed into a saver of lives and souls, attempting to rescue one after the other from Hades, but less for their sake than for my own. And despite all that, I could still so easily see myself as the inmate of an institution.

But, I tried to console myself, God knows my problems differ from those of my fellow inmates. All of them are retired, most of them are made of money, as one can tell from afar, or are at least armed with solid pensions, each like the other protected against all eventualities, these are people with backgrounds, their defect is of a definitive nature, so to speak, whereas I, now, temporarily unproductive and short of cash, am plagued with uncertainty, am therefore somewhat frightened, but for all that I'm still a long way off from being like them, from being retired; and right away I thought: if they knew that I, who possibly stand out a bit in this company—after all, I have no visible affliction, am by far the youngest person at the spa, and just from my appearance and manner am made of sterner stuff than anyone else here—if they knew that right now I'm broke and without anything to look forward to, but rather am for better or for worse staying here and vegetating, enjoying the swimming pool and hotel park simply on account of a gracious concession on the part of my old insurance company; if they knew that I, although not an invalid, am nevertheless a sort of charity case, a man experiencing an existential crisis, a parasite and con man, in other words; I only walk among you because of an act of mercy, my dear ladies and gentlemen, I murmured.

Was I struggling with writer's block at the same time as having a mid-life crisis? I scrutinized myself in the mirror of my plush bath-room, and looked away again immediately. And if I can't make it back with my old car, if the car breaks down, it'll soon be ready for the scrap heap, I said to myself, and caught myself thinking of a premature departure from the spa; but if I got a flat tire while fleeing, I wouldn't even be in a position to pay for the cost of the repair, let alone the cost of towing the car anywhere; and in any case, where should I flee to? There was a paying guest sitting in my Parisian apartment.

This Abano is hell, and now my rage was directed at the seventy-eight-year-old Herr Saurer, my fellow countryman, because he had confided in me, talking down to me, or so it seemed, that he was in the process of writing his memoirs. Oh yes, beautiful memoirs, I thought furiously, I'll show them beautiful memoirs, pure boredom, a fairy tale, pedantic, I thought, and envied him the writing of his memoirs, above all the peace he felt while writing, the considerable arrogance, the courage, the confidence.

If only this subject matter that I've been carrying around with me for so long now had finished its fermentation process; if only I had this state of inner turmoil behind me; if I could see the thing in front of me; if I had received my marching orders together with a map of my route; if only I could write again. Instead, I'm sitting around with this bunch of moribund old people and accepting the administration of daily fango packs as part of this "paid holiday."

And then I thought of several of my recurrent ideas of beauty; there was the radiance of gardens at dawn, walking along a narrow passageway between gardens, that feeling of intimacy; there was the feeling of happiness that came from being alone in a garden, when you catch your breath from sheer bliss.

And there was the continual colorful clanging of a port city, walking down to the harbor below the crooked walls of buildings that cast sharp, jagged shadows; I'm walking down deep in the rock, past the openings into the stores, past the caverns of the taverns, the taste of seaweed on my tongue and the sharp smell of the sea and the fish market in my nostrils; I'm walking down the pungent street with its sharp turns—where am I going? Into the adventure of a new horizon. Doors banging, bars, a young hooker standing in a dark doorway, departure in every sense of the word, with only the clothes on my back and otherwise nothing that belongs to me.

I tried to write that down at the small table in my hotel room with the curtains drawn to keep out the heat; I was writing in a dark, hot hotel cubicle where everything was varnished smooth with unfamiliarity. And in the adjacent bathroom I could contemplate my face, which now also seemed unfamiliar to me.

That Genoese with his pasty complexion and five o'clock shadow, whose skin always seems sweaty and unclean, with his dark, glowing eyes behind his glasses, and his arms with their thick covering of black hair; this Genoese preoccupied me, there was always a sort of young girl's smile affectedly engraved on his face, he pushed through the swinging door as if he wanted to make himself invisible, thereby achieving the exact opposite. He breathed a greeting at me, he studied the menu, he poured himself a glass of water, he ate, occasionally glancing up at the others from his usually downcast eyes. He didn't drink, didn't smoke, didn't talk.

And the sturdy Austrian women came in, plunked down in their chairs, put their arms on the table, and then they got their fruit juice, which they carefully, economically made last over the entire course of the meal; they took a little sip, then they waited for the main course, waited while the waiter raced here and there and sometimes let huge platters fall to the floor; they waited and waited while the others noisily ate their hors d'oeuvres, waited until the waiter had cleared away that course and raced in for the following act; they looked at the others with deliberate indifference, but it had a different effect, with all their feigned indifference, they were asking to be excused for their presence. One of them pretended to be engrossed in the menu, she was, as I noticed, the one who had the habit of crumbling the usually hard rolls into her meat and vegetables. Two of them always had sweets or ice cream for dessert, the third ate fruit and always packed up all the leftovers. When the bar pianist played during the candle-lit dinners the three of them clapped the loudest. But their leader, the one with the mania about the rolls, did so in a particular manner. She waited impassively until the piece came to an end, then she lifted her rounded lower arms and clapped like a jackhammer, continuing on after everyone else had stopped, she kept it up to the very end, she had the last word, that was *her* number, and now she had let everyone see that.

The masseur Antonio often spoke of *fare l'amore*; once he said, after the sexual act was completed, he always felt the urge to run away, he had to get away from the bed, even if just for as long as it took to smoke a cigarette. Why, I said, if it's beautiful, one can never have enough of it, why run off right away? Afterward, he said, he turned away, because a man, after completing the sexual act, *did not cut a good figure*; the women never went limp, they wanted to keep on going, in that, they were superior to the man, that was their strength. Antonio seemed to know everything about everyone. He started work at four in the morning and worked through until noon. He also massaged most of the women. He said the old ones, and especially the very old ones among them, sometimes bit him with their false teeth, they got quite wild from the massage. He said it good-naturedly. He was married and had two children. At the first ball, a handsome young man was present, he was a masseur in another hotel, the dancing, his business as a taxi dancer, was additional income. He danced imaginatively and at the same time with discipline, with his arm around a brazen woman in her mid-fifties who was behaving like a maenad. The pianist had made fun of the people who were dancing, as he sang, he wove insults and oaths into the texts of his torch songs. At one table, the female Austrian soldiers had sat at the ready; a fat Italian had fondled a compatriot oleaginously.

It was late at night when I arrived back in Paris, and even before going to my apartment, I climbed the hill to Sacré-Cœur. The city lay at my feet in ghostly illumination, vaguely glittering, whole sections glowing.

In the following days I climbed up to Sacré-Cœur in the mornings and the evenings, I went there as if I had to perform morning and evening prayers. I looked out over the hanging parks, embraced by staircases, the snowy mosque, the domes of the church behind it, looked out over the sea of buildings—to the bared teeth of the satellite in the hazy distance. But between the sea of buildings, sometimes it seemed to be a sea of glaciers, there was an icily shimmering stalactite landscape. On other days and at other hours the sea blossomed into thousands of breakers, those were the whitish, ocherous, gray backs, the backs of the walls with the slate-gray brows of their roofs, sometimes they emerged from purple clouds as from the pool of creation, and the white was the most spiritual white, a white like clown's make-up, like Chinese white. It was the endless city, and I remembered the streets and squares, their names, I remembered how it was down on the pavement and at the markets, I remembered the people, their stories, their fates being whispered by the stone.

I'll never get hold of you, don't turn me away, accept me: city, your prisoner.

BUT WHERE IS LIFE, I ASKED MYSELF ANXIOUSLY in my boxroom, sitting at my table with my view of the old dove man who now sent his doves over to me. Yes, it had recently begun to seem as though he was amusing himself by chasing the unwelcome doves in my direction with dismissive hand gestures. I didn't react.

Where was life? It was at the corner in the form of the people standing there; it was transported through the underground tunnels in the Metro and shoveled up into the light; it took me into its arms in the discreet rooms of the *maisons de rendez-vous*; it glided across the television screen; it hid itself in the city; it ran through my thoughts. But was I taking part in life? I shared neither the hopeless material circumstances of the immigrants in my neighborhood, nor the questions of the intellectuals in the brighter districts, I didn't take part anywhere, not even in the political life of this nation to which I did not belong, I didn't participate, I sat in the prison of my room, clung to paper, bent over my typewriter, intent on putting something down that would be lasting or at least would be seen, something I could hold on to. I often had the feeling that I wasn't so much living here as simply being allowed to live—just as the tramp on the bench passed water. And yet I had come here to win life.

Life is to be lost or gained, I had pretentiously maintained when I had met that girl who'd infected me with this love poisoning. It happened on a trip abroad, we had been introduced, and now we were sitting in a circle of people we knew and didn't know in a Greek bar, drinking and talking and drinking, and suddenly the girl I didn't know at all directed a request to me, say something, she said; I thought, what does she mean by *say*, what can I say to her, we barely know each other, good gracious, what does she mean. Say something, she repeated, and so I said, I have no idea why, that same sentence, I said, I think I have nothing to say, there is nothing to say, unless it's that life is to be lost or gained.

And in the same night we slept together, but I knew right away it was no affair, this was no passing affair, nor was it simply communication, a "conversation with our hands on the other per-on's body," no, it was destruction and revelation at the same time, I didn't know what was happening to me, but ever since then the word UNIO has been going around in my head, I don't know if this word was there because for the first time in my life I had experienced such a fusion, what's probably meant by the word "marriage," or whether it had only just occurred to me at that moment that there could really be such a thing. I drove home poisoned, and at home I told my wife what had happened to me, I had to say what was on my mind, because I knew that every cell of my physicality announced it with the utmost clarity, it couldn't be kept a secret, the entirety of my changed being expressed it.

I stood before my beloved wife and had to confess the dreadful truth. After that, we sat for nights confronted with our broken marriage. I cried with my wife, but I thirsted for my beloved so much that I had to see her again right away. We arranged to meet in Paris, and we spent three days in Hôtel du Paradis, Place Emile Goudeau. It was early spring, the room was awful, a narrow room with faded wallpaper, a door that hung crookedly and never really shut properly, a narrow bed and a curtain that billowed in the wind. I can still see the curtain in my mind's eye, I see the two of us in this room running to the window with our naked bodies, and from the window, looking out over the city, over the sea of buildings. I passed through all states in those nights, sometimes I woke up with a start and heard myself talking in a loud voice to my wife who had stayed behind, talking in our language, which my beloved did not understand. There was a mild wind blowing on those nights, an early spring arriving, the wind changing direction from one moment to the next. Once I looked out our window at two high attic windows in a building far-ther downhill, I just saw a part of each picture. In the one window, a studio window, I saw the powerful arms of a man eating and pouring himself a glass of wine, I just saw one corner of the table and part of the man who was eating, but it was still enough for me to be able to imagine that he was an artist, enjoying a late meal after finishing his work, and I imagined his studio with the equipment for his work, I imagined his working life, the simplicity, the honesty, the courage to live that way. In the other window, I saw an old man lying in bed, and at his side a child who was reading aloud to him from a book. These window pictures weren't hallucinations, these pictures of people in different stages of life, the sick man who might die soon and the creative artist, the two of them impressed themselves upon me, back then in PARADIS. That's what I saw, I, who was satisfying my hunger for a food that I hadn't even known existed until then.

We parted in the early morning at Gare de l'Est. It was raining, we walked silently side by side, like convicts. A few months later, I moved definitively to Rue Simart.

When I stood at the window of my boxroom and stared out into the courtyard, it was usually late at night when I stood there, because during the day I was afraid of closer contact with the old dove man, so I kept well back; when I stood at my open window and stared down into the now deathly quiet courtyard and at the cracked, disintegrating walls, I felt the pain of this love as a deprivation, as a gnawing pain in my heart, and I thought that this feeling was the most real, and thus the most precious, the strongest that I possessed. Let it run wild, but let it last, I thought.

Where is life? I had sighed in Zürich, when I sat at my ironing table and hammered away at my typewriter in the building with the two teachers and the hunchbacked Fräulein Murz; I thought, this lowly and subservient life in Zürich gets more worn out by the day and holds no more secrets for me; I thought, this worn-out life can't be all there is to living, and I dreamed of another country, of a scene where life would come at me like a thundering cavalcade on the street and trample me underfoot; and then it would touch me again, and I'd feel as I had in earlier years, when everything seemed full of miracles and adventures, pain and enlightenment.

I had given up my workroom in the building in the old part of the city with its hunchbacked genius loci, and had moved in with an artist in another district. The large studio, six-by-ten meters with windows high up, had been promised to me, but the painter was to have access to it until he could move to his new place; in the meantime, I was to make use of the adjoining rooms, which he offered to me so that these quarters, which I regarded as extremely desirable, would not be lost to me. I worked for almost an entire year with the painter in the studio. Until then, I had known him only by sight. He was called Karel S., had penetrating, sometimes slightly squinty eyes in a round, bearded face, was stocky, and carried the paunch of a heavy drinker in front of him.

Usually, I was home in our studio apartment before him, then the door opened, and Karel ambled silently in on his short legs and bear paws, carrying two bulbous Chianti bottles in his arms, four liters, his daily ration, but he didn't start with the wine right away, he put the bottles aside, went into the kitchen, where he brewed up some herbal tea for himself, poured a mouthful of herbal tea into a soup bowl with handles and then filled it up the rest of the way with wine, this mixture was his breakfast, but after he had drunk the blend, he carried on with wine alone until he was blind drunk and had his marvelous, pre-Christian, heathen sleep.

I liked Karel a lot, he was wise, he knew about medicinal herbs, spices, juices, and he got along well with animals. He could stick his arm up to the shoulder into a horse's mouth without getting bitten, and he bewitched or calmed the most vicious dogs by going right up to them with his penetrating gaze, and the dogs began to whine and lay down for him. Some of them started to lick his hand right away. Incidentally, he had this power not only over animals and plants but over people as well. It was wonderful living with Karel, he was extremely sensitive, neither coercing me to join him in his excessive drinking nor bothering me when I was working. When I sat at my big ironing table, I felt secure in the knowledge that my Karel was present in the next room, the gymnasium-sized painter's studio, between the paintings he was working on and all the countless, inexplicable pieces of equipment that make up a painter's household, whether he was painting or not, drinking or not, in his case I never had nasty situations like I'd had with poor Florian, and I would never even have entertained the thought that Karel should be working or not working, I paid no attention, whether he was producing anything or not: he was a Magus, in touch with the miraculous, he had a sixth through eighth sense, he could talk with every living creature and with dead things, and he could sleep like a master. He slept for months on end, and when his wife phoned, I became accustomed to lying, I said, he's just gone out on an errand, do you want him to call you back? His wife had a real fear of being stuck with an alcoholic for a husband, and when friends occasionally brought him home unconscious, or when he was dropped off in that state by a good-natured taxi driver, she sometimes locked him out, thinking that such measures would deter him, that she was doing him a service.

Karel's father had been a shoemaker and a drinker, had had a pet chicken and a pig who lived with him in his shoemaker's and drinker's workshop, keeping him company, and on the occasion of one family get-together, when not only the entire clan, but also the local Catholic priest were gathered together at the long table in the garden, the whole long table, set with the bowls and plates and glasses and food, suddenly tipped over, because the pig was trying to take its place at Karel's father's feet, it must have been a sizeable, pink, pinkish-gray pig.

Karel came from the country, he also knew mushrooms really well, and he knew about medicinal herbs, but for himself, that is, as far as alcoholism went, he knew of no cure, the mixture with the herbal tea didn't do a drop of good, and later on, Karel left us several times for withdrawal treatments, from which he returned as if from a fountain of youth, having lost his paunch, and with his skin looking as healthy as a young girl's, but the cure never lasted more than a few weeks, soon he took up his old habits again.

Downstairs in the building was a tobacco shop run by Fräulein Weishaupt. When I went into the shop, I always did my best to open the door carefully, so as not to hit it against the parrot's cage that stood on a rather high pedestal right inside the shop door. The parrot had one claw lifted up as high as its head, and its head tilted to one side, the better to scrutinize the newcomer. I breathed in the scents of the various tobaccos and spent a while browsing the paperback books in their stand, and then Fräulein Weishaupt came out of the back room and walked toward her customer, her small eyes blinking, she always gave that impression, as though she was coming out of the dark into blinding daylight. But the blinking had nothing to do with weak eyes, she blinked as she was sizing up the customer, and this kept him at a distance, it had more to do with skepticism and pride. Fräulein Weishaupt was a resolute person who had an arrogant streak. She studied people, and was always waiting for something extraordinary, but she only seldom found an interlocutor she considered worthy of hearing her own, that is Fräulein Weishaupt's, well-considered opinions. Besides having the parrot, she may have devoted herself to some passion or science, such as gambling or fortune-telling or spiritualism. But she was definitely also kind.

A few steps from our run-down building, which was already slated for demolition, there was a tall office building, and in front of it was a narrow island with a lawn and a few trees. This island of greenery, which looked like a doormat in front of the cold concrete colossus, was presumably left over from what had once been a park, which had been engulfed by the modern business fortress and covered over with concrete; I drew this assumption because of its massive old trees. It was the closest piece of greenery, and this leaf-green always made me pause for breath, I sucked my lungs full, especially when it was raining, I sucked the whole tree in, as if I could effectively stave off starvation due to lack of happiness. I don't know what kind of happiness that tree held, likely a childhood happiness, when

I looked up into the effervescence of young leaves, yes, let it rain, I thought, and sucked in the smell of the rain, there was something contagious about it, a note of alarm, there were no more chestnut trees like that around here, it was a universe of a tree, I stretched up toward the foliage that was scaled and layered in so many different ways, as I let the dog sniff the lawn; even more than the chestnut tree, my dog loved the cedar, he could never sniff the rough bark of its trunk long enough, and inside, behind the glass of the ground-floor rooms of the high-rise, I saw the distinguished computer programmers, both men and women, going about their business, and they probably noticed the man with the dog, perhaps even joked about him, or envied him the time and leisure to let his dog graze while he looked up into the planets of the leaves, where white candles were already growing.

At my table I often got that tormenting feeling of being deserted that one suffers as a child. Then I seemed to be in an adjoining room to life, cut off from everything. I got down to writing, it was as if I would only be capable of seeing, of breathing, of communicating by writing; as if the day I had not captured in writing had not been a day at all. *My day today will only be* my *day tomorrow if I recall it in a different setting.*

If I don't note things down, everything remains unreal, I thought. Being in a foreign country can take possession of me in such a threatening manner that I fear I'll gradually die in the midst of life. Taking notes was both a desire to write myself into something, as well as a desire to write myself out of something: out of being split off, and into life. I abandoned myself to the language, the sentences, the parlando, as to a sleigh that would carry me there.

The fear of dying also explains that other urge which occasionally causes me to drift off course, not only into an outer life, but also into the life of a drinker, into a life of destruction and self-destruction, it's a danger, this urge is the urge to deaden my senses. Is it the fear of falling away from what feeds me, that is, from contemplation? Is it necessary for the pendulum to swing between this getting out to let life hit me over the head (until it reverberates like the edge of a forest in summer, as if a tuning fork had been hit) and then the retreat back inside, must the outer wasteland alternate with the inner tomb? The act of climbing up, as if from the depths, coated with mud, hung with algae . . . Does one *have to* attain a state of drunkenness, a state of drowning, a state of emergency, in order to really write? Do I always have to have a crisis first?

Life is to be lost or gained. I'm looking for it. When I say I'm looking for life, I mean that I'm looking for what it takes to be alive, to be awakened, for the awakening, yes, the awakening! To be awakened from the state of someone fighting for reality in the midst of chaos or apprehension, ennui, melancholy, hopelessness, lethargy. I throw myself into life as I cling to my writing, and in the sense of someone begging to be wrapped up in life, to be flooded with it, awakened, distracted from my writing yet again; and then I am distracted from life by collecting things to write about to restore my self-confidence. I flee a few steps out into life because I'm afraid of being cooped up in my room, and outside I long to be writing because I'm concerned about my source of income.

I sit in this boxroom as if on standby. Waiting.

I've just applied dubbin to my two favorite suitcases. The one, Bassano's old leather suitcase, as I've called it, comes from London, or, more precisely: from a store for "lost property" in Bloomsbury, I bought it in 1968, specifically because of its unique, long and narrow shape, it looks like an instrument case, has a width of about the German Industrial Standard A4 paper size, which is 220 by 297 mm, but it also looks like a maidservant's small suitcase, especially when it's opened, the inside is lined with gray ticking. It was badly scratched, but the leather was of a quality that inspired trust. Over the years, it has nevertheless become rather dilapidated, it started disintegrating, turning into dust, especially at the corners and edges, which is why, when I carried it around with me, my pant legs were always covered with red dust, as if I had waded through knee-high pollen. Finally, it fell apart at the seams, literally. I recently had it patched up, now the seams are reasonably strong, and since I've applied dubbin to it, it's shiny and smooth. I'm attached to the thing in an almost superstitious way.

I purchased the other manuscript case even earlier, in 1965 I think, on Bahnhofstraße, Zürich's main drag, in an old, established leather-goods store by the name of Lilian that was having a clearance sale, it was at a time that I was in dire financial straits. Maybe I didn't need a case, but it was probably necessary to maintain my defiant attitude, I borrowed the money and spent it on this luxury item that was made to last, I invested in a life on the move and sneered at security.

While I was applying the dubbin to my suitcases, the old dove man kicked up more of a racket than usual, probably to draw attention to himself. He doesn't like it when I disappear out of his field of vision. Perhaps I've long since become part of the old man's routine, perhaps keeping an eye on me is now part of his daily work.

The suitcases belong to my mobile household. I've carried manuscripts around in them for years, I feed, indeed line the cases with paper until they're crammed full of it, and one day, if I'm lucky, everything goes into a book, the papers leave the suitcases, the book slips out of Bassano—just as I would like to imagine myself slipping out or going forth from this inner subterranean tomb, the writing of this book, as a different or a new person.

When I purchased the two cases, I lived in a small room not far from Zürich's Bahnhofstraße, wall-to-wall with foreign workers from Italy, whose cooking late in the evening filled my room with a wonderful aroma, an aroma that mixed with the aroma from the cheese store on the main floor. At that time, I always wrote at night, because by day I was in pursuit of survival jobs at the newspaper. My window looked out on a renowned old beerhouse and restaurant, I could overhear the closing of the place, the bawling of the last drinkers, and early in the morning the awakening of the street under the foot-steps of people who worked the early shift, from time to time the pleasant sounds of the city street-sweeper truck that sprayed water everywhere, and sounds of the café up the block being readied for business. Before I went to bed, I would take myself and my dog out for a walk. One of the foreign workers from Italy had lost the toes on one of his feet when someone drove over them, and since then he limped, but he didn't complain when he told me about it, on the contrary, he seemed to be happy about it, because since the accident he had received a disability pension and easier work and, all in all, it was an improvement.

I've rented a lot of rooms or adjoining rooms like that, they enabled me to get around well in the city, and even in the world. They were always equipped with the same few things I needed for my work, and I never spoke about them to anyone because I wanted the ghosts that haunted them to stay put, or, to be precise, the work-ing atmosphere. The rooms were also cases for my works in progress, and when the work was finally finished, the case was abandoned, its skin was shed. Once I had a henhouse overlooking Lake Zürich, an advertising agent had converted it into a studio, complete with shower and kitchenette, stylish, and the sleeping quarters were on a built-in second floor. The whole front wall was made up of windows looking out on the lake, but in spite of that, it was still obviously a henhouse, standing in the midst of other such coops, someone had previously run a poultry farm there. One time the water main broke in the studio-coop, the floor was under water, and the cat who always visited me during the day had jumped up onto my worktable to save herself; I didn't know where the shut-off valve was located and ran over to the nearby factory, which was no longer in operation, instead it housed a commune, mainly women and children, the men went to work during the day, or to the university; by chance, one of them was home and came to my aid.

I'm no producer of books, not a book person at all, I complain to Beat. The books are only what I leave behind me, I creep through my books into the light or onto land, I say. When the book appears, I've already passed that stage, do you follow?

Just forget about it, says Beat, why not, no one is forcing you to write books, why don't you just drop the whole thing?

All the same, I say to Beat, all the same, there's always this sense of a mission, or better, an expedition that drives me on, and then there's also the feeling of being underway once I start working on the book. But up to that point . . . Until I've reached that state . . . it's . . .

Like carrying a child to full term, says Beat, go ahead and say it, if you have to allude to pregnancy.

It takes a damn long time, I think, before a bit of subject matter, something I've experienced, has been adequately shaken and fermented in the camel's hump, that is, until it's probably been digested, so that finally, maybe after ten years, it rises up as vivid material and becomes accessible. But until then, it stays in the dark, and it makes me really sick.

My problem is that I go along so knee-deep in a fog, so terribly in the dark, I say. What's worse: I feel like I'm being buried alive, and I write to dig my way out. I try to pull myself out by the thread of my writing.

Now you're going to have to explain yourself, says Beat. You mean, you can't make up a story, or you don't want to? Or do you have nothing to say, my friend? Why must you so absolutely have to see yourself as a hagiographer? If it's an obsession, you know, a fixation, you could still be helped. You could go to a psychiatrist, damn it.

I say, Beat, I say, my only problem is that I don't write about what I already know but rather to find something out; I get going on something unknown or subconscious, which is not to be confused with fantasy; I have to grope my way toward it, have to make contact. I have to sound out the terrain, if I knew what was going on, I wouldn't have to write at all. My problem is scraping together the material, the preparatory process, not the packaging. As far as I'm concerned, I don't think this can be explained to anyone who isn't in the same line of work. And now I think, when it comes right down to it, I can only begin writing the book fermenting in me when I catch the scent of its most secret theme. When the thing reveals its identity, as it were, with its pulse, its body odor, its weight, its invisible life. When I smell it. Its most secret theme is not the essence of my own experience, it's that part of it I can share with others, also with books, yes, it's like a memory one can no longer place, something very old or ageless. There's something legendary about my material that I can at most enshroud and wrap up, perhaps omit, but never express. It doesn't appear in the plot or the action, it will swirl away or be silent on a lower level, and perhaps rise up from the whole like a mixture of scents.

It will be in the sentences. And I run after myself in my sentences in order to catch up with it. That's when I feel as if I'm walking on the paper or on the water like a water strider. But what doesn't find its way into a sentence in this sleepwalking fashion remains paper, mere paper, it's a stillbirth and not worth mentioning.

A book, I thought recently, as I climbed the steps of Rue Becquerel to Sacré-Cœur, has to be as removed from its author, from the writer's biography, his storehouse of ideas, as a soap bubble that frees itself from its wand and sails through the air, shimmering prismatically, intriguingly. A book has to smell like a memory. So much so that whenever the book, or some part of it, or even just its ambience comes to mind, the reader can no longer be certain where it came from; it's become personal, become part of the reader, it moves you from within, stretches out its feelers. What was that, the reader wonders. What am I remembering now? It has become a part of your past. That's how it has to be, I shout at Beat, *dissolved in the stomach of memory.*

Why are you yelling at me, are you out of your mind? asks Beat, who is stretched out on my sofa, leafing through a newspaper. He has an unlit cigar between his teeth, one of those long, thin things, which he, a nonsmoker out of principle, permits himself to enjoy only after his cognac.

Or might it be possible that my writing touches upon life only glancingly, at best, that it remains on its surface. And is it that I hope to be able to get along some day without it, without these aids, without crutches like this, by which I mean, without writing?

Are you still meditating on writing, asks Beat. Why not simply regard it as a business, he says. Look at it as a business or a skilled trade.

A business, I think, that's well put. But what am I to do with my business during those horribly long incubation periods? When my income dwindles and then runs out, simply ends, just as a fire goes out; but the bills don't stop, they arrive with their own peculiar regularity, they pile up on the table or in a drawer, and then come the reminders, the threatening letters; and still no prospect of money, where is it going to come from? And I see nothing but bills, I start calculating how much I owe to everyone and how long I can possibly hope to defer payment. People who have no money should go out and work, not study. They should work, said my Uncle Alois, even if they have to sweep up horse dung (as he said back then).

And now I'm starting to see everything in the light of those bills, those unpaid bills that are floating to the surface of my consciousness like corpses in a lake; I sum up my life and arrive at the most discouraging result—a deficit that can never be made up, it seems to me that my whole life has been spent in the red; I think of the effort, despair, illusions that my books have cost me, I see my life as a failure, but then also as a presumptive fraud; if you're never in the money, you're not worth much, says the Robber in Robert Walser's novel, and: a person who has no money is a wretch. They're right, the people who think that way, I tell myself at such moments; I feel guilty when I think of them, also of the Arabs and other minorities in my quarter. Even as a child, I felt ashamed of my contemplative nature.

All the fears and doubts I've ever had about living as a writer come creeping out and destroy my confidence.

Beat is of the opinion that the business of writing is basically no better and no worse than any other business, a skilled trade like every other one; like that of the cabinet-maker next door, he thinks, or pretends that's what he thinks; and as with the cabinet-maker, the only thing that matters is the quality of the work produced, as far as he's concerned: the degree of quality, of perfection, nothing more; it's simply ridiculous to claim that society ranks writers higher and has some sort of special sympathy for them.

If I went along with Beat, I'd say that books are the products of a craftsman, meant to be used; if I should say to myself, books are devoured or deciphered with difficulty, they entertain, educate, denounce, enlighten, amuse, please; they blossom for a season and retreat back into the bookcase, along the wall of books, where they become just another furnishing, like the chest of drawers made by the cabinet-maker, like the wall-hanging; or else they become cultural possessions; that's all well and good, I guess . . . but how do I reconcile this view with the irrational, sometimes dreadful conditions in which the books were written, with these other costs? And what about the less-visible aspects of the question, the vitality of certain books, how they captivate, take one's breath away; the depth, the explosive, life-bringing force, the *life*, that distinguishes a book, if it's a genuine book, from others, and which it continues to deliver, to radiate, even when it's gone back on the shelf? That's a question that can be left to the reader; certainly *you* don't need to bother yourself about it, I told myself. Just do your work, do it as well as you can.

I say, Beat, I say, it's clear that one is inclined to overrate this wretched business, above all because it's such lonely one; and one would like to consider a life lived in service of this particular function as unique, one would like to see one's own person as standing apart, and why not. Furthermore, I am in no way accountable to you, *I* am the organizer and owner of this enterprise, I bear the risk, although I by no means despise cabinet-makers and office workers as a result.

And someone like you chose freedom, sneers Beat. You're

oversensitive! he says. My God, writers!

And now I think about how I sometimes lean over the counter in the noise of a bustling bar, people talking and playing pinball, and I become lost in thought, it's beautiful standing there like that, at a bar, surrounded by the *city*, and how I suddenly start to *see*, to feel, to murmur, and the fish are jumping; and now I *know* that by virtue of this waiting and walking and dreaming, this journey, I will be able to preserve some of what I experience—but when these functions fail, and everything seems dead in me, and I have really nothing more to show than this freedom, which now looks as if it's the freedom to throw everything away, or to fall by the wayside; and I get scared, and I picture myself appealing to a foundation for the arts for assistance; I would direct my request to the administrator, and with reference to my business I would ask for support, for immediate aid, if possible, urgently, it is urgent, most honored sir, I might add; and I would receive the answer: very well, we will examine your case, but we request that you in the meantime exercise some patience, you must understand that we have to think of everyone, even of the cabinet-makers, florists, Trappists, of everyone who is creating culture, not just you . . . Stop it, I say to myself, books are a gift, even if they have to be made and above all lived.

Life is getting ever more virtuosic, and a person is like a cello; it doesn't play if it isn't touched by the artist's bow. I read something like that in Maxim Gorky, I think.

I still hadn't reached the point where I could start working on my book, but I kept on as before, making notes as a warm-up exercise, to keep in practice, and I let the fish jump when I went for my walks, and when I was back home again, I tried to remember the jumping of the fish in my thoughts, sometimes I ran right back outside again IN SEARCH OF A LOST FISH, but then I sat down at my typewriter and let the carriage run back and forth as I ran after the sentences, letting it flow until the spring tide had passed.

I'm really not chasing after life here; if anything, I'm chasing after words, at present I'm a seeker of words, but where is life, I ask myself

and then I dreamed that I was riding on a train, I found myself in the same compartment as other writers and said to the man sitting next to me, I have recently discovered that when tying my shoelaces I can hear what's being said somewhere far away, I've found that I can listen to my shoelaces as I would listen to a tape recorder, and while I'm staring into the face of the man next to me, which at first shows disbelief, then an indulgent smile, I hear myself continuing, it's unbelievable, totally unbelievable, isn't it, but it's true. This supernatural ability fell right into my lap, I could hardly fail to notice it; I was doing something as ordinary as tying my shoes, after all. And right after that, I dreamed that I could swing and fly through the air with the help of a piece of paper. I no longer know exactly how I managed from a standing position to swing myself up into the air with the piece of paper in my hands, but, in any case, I could do it in my dream and tried it again and again, every time with success, and then I was flying, hanging down from my piece of paper, I held on to it as if I was hanging from a dragon, at a height of two thousand meters above a landscape large enough to contain three whole countries, it was a gigantic territory, my territory, and the landscape was a hilly, early spring greenish brown or brownish green, a lonely region, an abandoned and more likely Swiss than French landscape, I could see it effortlessly, from my bird's-eye view, I had the overview, and at the same time not even the slightest sign of life down below escaped me; and then later on, after I had landed and was walking normally again, on my two feet, I happened to meet up with a crowd of people who must have been journalists, reporters, who had gathered here for an important occasion, and now I recognized my dear friend Beat in one of the groups, he too was a reporter, I went up to him, although he waved me away, annoyed, he had no time, so I quickly jotted down the miracle that had happened to me on a notepad, writing down the news, I'm not sure why, probably because I was in high spirits, in the form of an uneven quatrain, tore the page from my notepad, and slipped it to him, I *had* to tell someone about it, and later, when Beat finally had time for me, he said this quatrain really wasn't anything surprising, it wasn't well written, and thematically of little interest, he didn't even comprehend my message, he had taken it for a poem, unable to think of anything except as a reporter, or so he appeared in my dream.

So I dreamed of miracles or of wonderful talents, and when I asked myself about the meaning of these dreams, I had to think of writing right away. I thought, the only thing this can mean is that the trick with the paper and the feat with the shoelaces have something to do with writing. But why do my shoelaces, of all things, let me hear what is being said somewhere else, and probably not just at some local, spatial remove, but also in a different time, in the past? Well, I said to myself, with your shoes you've already wandered and walked and now roamed a considerable way through life, they've probably stored these voices, they haven't forgotten, to some extent they're carrying them along after you; if you're humble enough, they'll share it with you. You have to bend down, you have to bend down to yourself, then you'll be able to hear it.

And as far as the flying is concerned, that can probably only mean that by virtue of this piece of paper and what you undertake or manage to do with the paper, you can gain not only insights, but also overviews and outlooks that you wouldn't otherwise have, you let your eyes wander over a vast terrain by holding fast to the paper, you're like the hawk circling over a gray landscape, and when something moves, it swoops down and grabs that thing with its talons, you can grasp what's alive by virtue of this sailing circling, you just have to want to do so, at least that's what the dream means, I tell myself.

I was certainly no interpreter of dreams, at least I hadn't seriously attempted it until then, but recently, in fact ever since I've been here in Paris, alone in my boxroom, and waiting for my book, but also for the girl to reappear, my dream life has been extraordinarily rich and eventful, it's even seemed to me that my dreams were speaking to me very directly, as if they wanted to help me, yes, I had slept a lot and dreamed a lot, and maybe it was because of my dreams that I had gone to bed so often in the middle of the day or the afternoon

and now another dream occurred to me: I found myself high up on a very wobbly scaffolding, it was a scaffolding made up of several makeshift racks piled on top of each other, and besides that, it was on wheels, a high, fragile scaffolding, and I was on top of it, which meant I had made a mistake climbing up this thing, exactly how I'd done it was unclear to me, but it was very clear that I'd never get back down again without risking my neck, I was in mortal danger; I was afraid, and was thinking, as I cautiously peered over the edge and down into the depths: I'll plunge to my death from this wobbly tower; I'm not going to get out of this alive, I thought, already starting to panic, and at the same moment I recognized that not far away, within arm's reach, was a window ledge, I reached out and managed to pull the whole wobbly tower, with me on top of it, over to this white window ledge; I'll hold fast to it, I thought, and then suddenly a big window opened inward, nearby, and in the window stood one of my oldest friends; it'll be easier this way, he said, climb in, and I climbed into the BUILDING.

I said to myself: how on earth did I get onto this wobbly scaffolding, I must have *gotten lost while climbing*, and also, was I so blind that I didn't even know that a building and a friend and help was near at hand. That could easily have resulted in my death, I thought, but in the end, I had *climbed in*, but where? into the building; or just into an inhabited floor of the building, where my friend lived? in any case, I was no longer alone.

What can that have to do with my book, I wondered again. Could it be that I was so lost while climbing, so off course that I kept waiting for the beginning of my book or my "marching orders" to be handed to me on a plate when I'd already long since made a start in my daily writing exercises, with this warm-up writing, I had already climbed into life, all kinds of lives, into a world, a world of memory, largely, stations of a journey, and even if *I* hadn't realized, my foot, which had already set out on this path, the foot that had stepped over the border into freedom, had not forgotten. I can still be a part of it if I just bend down far enough, and if I use my paper to fly off from this spot I call my room: if I just let myself go, flow, fly, sleep, and dream.

Seen that way, I could even imagine that I'm not alone at all, at least not in my thoughts, not in the ones that ignited my writing and had it burn along this safety fuse

and as for the book, hadn't I already, several times already, dreamed that such a book lay before me without my having had the slightest idea that it existed, without my having the slightest idea of how it had come into being? Once, it was at a reading, in a bookstore, that I discovered, among many new releases laid out on a table, a book by me, just lying there, a new book, and it stood out a mile, insofar as it was mainly pieced together out of manuscripts, albeit between two covers, it was a combination of typescript and properly printed and published pages, all in a bundle, and there were handwritten pages too, it was a heterogeneous thing, and consisted of exactly 146 pages, and it had obviously been published, even if that had happened without my knowledge, and now it existed, and with some embarrassment, and at the same time joy, I took note of it, in my dream.

And there was another time that I found a new book by me in a bookstore, it was a tiny thing, and when I opened it, I saw it was an illustrated book, but the text and the pictures had been printed on the same pages, the beginning lines of the text were legible, I read them, read them out loud in amazement to someone else, but as it went on, the lines became increasingly inundated by the surging waves of the illustrations, I tried everything to retrieve them, but the words always sank below the surface.

Was that too an indication that I had already written something without knowing it? In my warm-up writing exercises, I had written rather indiscriminately, the main thing was to be writing, for me, *that* was as necessary as breathing. And now I thought, I'm right, my dreams are right, those sessions when the words bubbled out of me had already attracted all kinds of figures, my room is a real dove-cote sometimes, and by doves I mean thoughts, those whirling, wail-ing creatures that echo through my head, there's often a humming sound, as in a beehive, so really my room is quite populated, I should read up on this phenomenon sometime, I thought, but I didn't take the time to do so, the main thing is, you're writing

let it bubble, like the gutters bubble here in Paris, I still loved these gurgling, gushing grates, they don't exist in Switzerland, but they do here in Paris, and I've often stood and observed them, even when I was a boy, when I used to visit my aunt, when Paris was still my aunt's Paris, I had often stared in awe at those gurgling holes, and also at the usually black street sweepers with their wonderful brooms, when they swept the sputum and trash down from the sidewalk, toward the cleansing water that was bubbling out of the holes they had opened, directing it down into the sewers.

For me, the bubbling and gurgling was a wonderful sound, it would be nice to have a mouth that bubbled like that. The idea of a mouth spitting words and sentences appealed to me, no: of being or being able to become a gurgling mouth. It would be like an oratory; or a broadcasting station, a transmitter? Maybe that's the meaning of your emigration, maybe that's what you're about; maybe you had to let yourself be oppressed by this city until the gurgling began and now you're overflowing, be grateful for the oppression. You're afraid that life is passing you by outside, but perhaps there is no other life.

But, I tell myself, in my room I can only remember the other, the past life. What happened long ago is reaching me now. Now it has overtaken me. Its ruins roll to the threshold of my present day like a message in a bottle rolling up on a beach. And while I'm collecting all kinds of life here, and that is: past life!—while I'm preoccupied with it, it is "my life"—there is already a new life taking place, to which I as yet have no access.

I am the son of my father and my mother, I say to myself, the product of this meeting and mating, both their worlds flow together in me, and God knows, the two of them, for their part, were messengers from different, far distant ends of the earth; I am their product, just as I am the product of a long history and also the product of everything that has ever influenced me; I am saturated with thousands of things, a sum of hovering particles, teeming and whirling, and I am a responding, corresponding instrument; I'm connected with everything, whether I know it or not, after all, I'm just the innkeeper, and what does an innkeeper know . . . but when I occupy myself with these listening devices, I can receive things and pass some of them on, I'm writing to communicate something of what gives me a foothold.

Well then, get writing, I hear my dear friend Beat say to me in my thoughts, your life, as I now realize, can only be reached through writing, so what's the fuss, get down to it, and accept the fact.

I say, Beat, I say, life consists of what a person thinks in the course of the day, at least that's what I read, I think Emerson said it, it's his sentence, though it's horrible to go along with it, I'd rather life were in my shoes and I could scratch it off the soles and untie it with my shoelaces.

This dream, I'm writing it down late at night, still here in my boxroom, somewhat tired, while in Lebanon the Syrians are attacking the Israelis and the Israelis are attacking the Syrians, and while in France the increasingly embittered election campaign is coming to a head; while the stock market is crumbling; and now I remember that Brisa phoned me recently, her voice sounded crackly through the receiver, there are always these disruptions, I don't know if the problem is in my telephone, lately there's been more and more crackling and rustling on the line, I should have someone come to check it; my conversation with Brisa got interrupted before I understood what she wanted to say; I'd actually like to fly to Rio, if I could, I once heard that there's no problem with racism in Brazil because everyone is biracial anyway, I don't know if that's true; Brazil, I think, must be beautiful, but I thought that about East Asia too, before I actually arrived there, and now I see myself in the airplane, we are en route from Singapore to Medan, Sumatra, seen from the airplane this island kingdom really took on character, the islands, small islands, bridging islands looked like bubbles of steam and specks of fat, like plasma in the boiling soapy water of the ocean, they sprinkled the surface of the sea in lovely curves and roundels, a roundelay of creation, it was like a lesson about the origin of the earth out of the depths of the sea, let there be a firmament in the midst of the waters, these small landmasses pulsated in the aura of their torrid, hazy pall, as in the book of Genesis, and sparkled up to us, to the people flying overhead in a stifling hot crate. The pilot fiddled lazily with his instruments, when he hadn't simply flopped back into his seat, we could watch him when we weren't looking down onto this oceanic scene, onto this part of the globe where the stories by Joseph Conrad and Somerset Maugham are set, and then I fell asleep and dreamed of a wild rose, a single, unassuming rose that was blooming on a wall of my childhood, and when I woke up in our crate of a plane that was pitching and tossing high up in the air, and hot as a greenhouse inside, when I regained consciousness, I still had this image from my dream before my eyes, and I held fast to it like an amulet while we were descending and land thrust itself under our wings, it was the steaming top of the jungle in a haze of heat, then forests of palm trees, now and then I saw bits of corrugated metal gleaming up out of this tangle of green, those were huts or settlements, and when we landed, I saw ourselves surrounded by palm trees, nothing but straggly palm trees, it looked as though we were being greeted by dancing warriors in skirts of leaves; and there was this light, this humming interior lighting, as if one was on the inside of a lamp, a relentless light that illuminated everything, I'd soon had enough of it, so I started to long to be back in Europe; maybe I'd feel that way in Brazil too, and why go to Brazil, I think, you're in Paris and here you'll stay, I say to myself as I look out at the old dove man, who will leave the stage very soon now, by which I don't mean that he's going to die, God forbid, but that he will disappear from the window, I think he goes to bed shortly after eight in the evening, just as he's already up before six in the morning, it's inexplicable to me why he does that, my mother too always gets up that early in her senior's apartment, although she could sleep in now to her heart's content, you have *all the time* in the world, I tell her, but she doesn't like to hear that

while the dove man says good-bye to his favorite dove for the night, and while from the other windows facing the courtyard the televisions, the kitchen noises, many different voices, screams, laughter, and various kinds of music come together to create our regular evening racket, for some it's cacophony, but not for me, I'm writing down this dream in which I find myself standing in a magnificent apartment with high ceilings and big windows, the windows and the balcony doors are open, I'm standing in the light of a September morning, and now I suddenly know that I'm in Spain; I'm standing there, still very young, and watching an older man who's about forty, he's dark, slim, careful in his movements, and he's in the process of preparing for a trip; just now he's putting his suitcases beside an armchair, they're the most beautiful suitcases I've ever seen, made of blond calfskin, soft and sumptuous, and they have big, soft side pockets and straps; I'm standing there, not doing anything, but I'm waiting, not exactly for orders, but still waiting to take action, because the energetic man is the KING, and I'm, well, what exactly am I? I don't really know, I'm something between a secretary and a close friend, not really in his employ, but not just a guest either, something in between; I'm standing there, waiting, in the very sunny room with the cool air coming in, and now the *king* speaks, in a very quiet but firm voice, he asks me to please look after the goldfish in the aquarium during his absence, and don't forget to feed it, he says; and later, when I'm alone, I discover that the aquarium has tipped over and is empty except for the goldfish, it's lying motionless on the light-colored little stones, lying on its side, I'm shocked by my inattentiveness, I place the aquarium upright again, it immediately fills up with water, and lo and behold, the big goldfish moves, recovers, and starts slapping against the upper surface of the water with these rapid splashes, its mouth protruding

that was lucky, once again things turned out well, and now I think, what would have happened if it had just lain there and not come back to life? and now it occurs to me that I had recently received some *glad tidings* from someone I didn't know, it was late, I'd been at the movies in Clichy, and now I was going home along Rue Caulaincourt, under the trees, their canopies of leaves shining magnificently in the dark, I was almost walking on tiptoe so as not to break the magic spell of the quiet street, and at the one bar that was always open until late in the night, I had a whiskey brought to me outside, I sat facing the darkness of the street, and behind me was the bar, it seemed as though it must be sweltering in there because it was so bright and busy, of course it also seemed to shine like that because everything all around it was submerged in the silence of the night; inside several tipsy regular customers were laughing at one of their own who was trying to talk English with a foreign woman, a tourist, who was playing pinball. I sat at my little table outside, and these bursts and then waves of laughter came at intervals, I was happy, I was at home here, in my district, and I didn't want to go back to the apartment yet; then a man came up to me out of the darkness and laid an envelope beside my glass, on the envelope I read the words

M^r & Mme	[Dear Sir or Madam
Je suis sourd-muet	I am a deaf and dumb person
et vous présente	and in an appeal to your generosity
Le »Message du Bonheur«	I am presenting you with a
à votre bon cœur	"Message of Good Fortune"
Prix : I Fr. Merci!	Price : 1 franc. Thank you!]

and then I opened the envelope, after I had paid the asking price, a one-franc coin, and on the folded paper I read the announcement

Révélation du Destin   [Revelation of your Destiny]

and when I unfolded the paper, the following text:

Vous êtes d'une nature indécise, c'est- à-dire que vous ne savez jamais quoi faire, un rien vous embarrasse, ce qui est le plus fort c'est que vous voulez tout faire à la fois. Toujours plusieures idées en tête, vous ne savez pas laquelle entreprendre et cette indécision vous a déjà causé beaucoup d'ennuis dans la réussite de vos projets. Vous avez une bonne idée en tête, suivez-là jusqu'à complète réussite sans vous occuper d'autre chose et le succès est certain.

Vous avez dans votre existence une personne vous aimant beaucoup et il est mal heureux pour vous que vous ne partagiez pas ses sentiments.

Comme vous êtes très agréable en société, vous avez l'estime de votre entourage et tout le monde aime votre société.

[You are by nature indecisive, that is to say, you never know what to do, you make mountains out of molehills, and the worst part of it is that you want to do everything all at the same time. You always have several ideas in your head, and you don't know which one to attempt, and this indecision has already made it very difficult to succeed in your projects. You have a good idea in your head, follow it through to completion without getting distracted by other things, and you are sure to succeed.

There is someone in your life who loves you very much, and it is unfortunate for you that the love is not reciprocated.

Since you are a very pleasant person to be with, your friends hold you in high regard, and everyone appreciates your company.

RÉSUMÉ	SUMMARY
Caractère: Enjoué, plutôt bon, même trop confiant.	Character: Playful, quite kind, and even trusting.
Famille: Nombreuse, dont une partie fera sa carrière dans l'armée.	Family: Large, some of whom will have careers in the army.
Amour: Beaucoup de chance pour vous et pour ceux qui vous aimeront.	Love: You are very lucky, as will be those who love you.
Jeu: Assez de chance, main surtout pas trop d'entêtement.	Gambling: Lucky enough, but especially when you don't get carried away by it.
Jours de chance: le 9 et le 1.	Your lucky days: the 9th and the 1st.
Existance heureuse et vieillesse tranquille.	You will have a long and happy life.
Votre porte-bonheur sera: l'Opale.	Your lucky charm is: the opal.]

I thought this guy knew me astonishingly well, at least the most important things about me, and now of course I was even happier than before; such a heavenly evening is usually only possible in a dream, I told myself, so much flows through such an evening, an evening tailor-made for the flow of thoughts, I ordered another whiskey

and now I'm thinking of my mother and how nice it would be for her if I could treat her to a meal here, she always says, when I visit her, you are the only ray of light in my life, she says, and some day, you'll see, I'll come to visit you in Paris, Paris, she says, is the city of my dreams, it always has been, and then she tells me of *her* visits to her aunt, that was at the beginning of the 1930s and even before that, when she, a stylishly dressed young woman, wore the most elegant shoes of that time, and traveled repeatedly to Paris, and that aunt also had a little dog, its name was Fleurette, and at the last, it was short of breath and fat, I knew both the little dog and this aunt, who was my great-aunt, and when she was almost eighty, she moved to Bern to live with us, she had lost her husband in Paris after a long life, he had been a pharmacist and an officer of the Legion of Honor; but I'll probably never see my mother here, I think, how could I, how could she get around here on her legs, on which she comes running with such stiff little steps to the door when I ring her doorbell, she could neither get down to the subway, nor climb up onto the bus, and a long train trip or car ride is quite out of the question, but she probably sees it differently; and I think I'd also like to have my dog here, but I wouldn't dare to bring him, where could he run loose here, and, God knows, I wouldn't be able to take him out for a walk every evening here, and into the open, which is what he was used to, I thought of my tiny apartment and the different customs here, I was afraid, so I left him with friends back in Switzerland, he had it good with them, he had a garden, and his master was a retired gentleman who spoiled him, but my dog didn't last much longer, he died soon afterward; Florian had also gotten along well with my dog, not to mention Karel; but Beat didn't particularly like him, he doesn't like dogs, he finds that people who have dogs are people who like to dominate others, he rubbed that in several times; I don't ever want to have another dog, I'm my own dog, but I found Beat's arguments superficial and heartless, and now I'm reminded of my first dog, whom I had to have shot shortly before my final exams in high school, he was fourteen years old and had edema, could hardly stand on his legs anymore, and so I took him to the animal hospital one day, the attendant told me to bring my dog, who was resisting, into this shooting chamber, I said, here boy, heel, I said, and saw the dog overcoming his reluctance because he trusted me, he followed me, and when we were inside, he laid his old head against my knee, then the attendant gunned him down, my dog was still wagging his tail as he died, they handed over his collar and leash to me, and I set off for home with the two items.

I don't know why I'm writing all this, that was a lifetime ago, but there is no past, sometimes I dream of my first dog, just as I dream of my second, who was called FLEN and was held in high regard by Karel: Flen is a lord, Karel had said, but I don't need to dream of him, because I recognize him again in all dogs, the way dogs express themselves poses no problem for me, I think I understand the language of all dogs, because I myself had dogs, I know why they yawn at certain times, and what it means when they raise their hackles, I understand them; nothing is past, not even the pain, even if the cause of it has been cancelled out by the passage of time, I still see the masks of pain as clearly as if they were displayed in glass cases, everything is there, and everything is as if I had just dreamt it;

and now Beat comes in, addressing me as an author, he says, well, he says, have you finally successfully gotten through your rites of initiation, *mon écrivain*?

I say, Beat, I say, I'm tired. And I think: "WHY ARE ALL OF YOU MAKING SO MUCH NOISE WHEN YOU CAN SEE, CAN'T YOU, THAT I'M SLEEPING."

PARIS, 1977–1981

PAUL NIZON was born in Bern in 1929. After a career as an art historian and critic, he turned to writing full time in 1962, and moved to Paris in 1977, where he still resides. His work has won numerous awards, including the prestigious Austrian State Prize for European Literature in 2011.

JEAN M. SNOOK is Professor of German at Memorial University in St. John's, Newfoundland. She was awarded both the inaugural Austrian Cultural Forum Translation Prize in 2009 and the Wolff Translator's Prize in 2011.

SELECTED DALKEY ARCHIVE TITLES

SELECTED DALKEY ARCHIVE TITLES

HENRY GREEN, *Back.*
Blindness.
Concluding.
Doting.
Nothing.
JACK GREEN, *Fire the Bastards!*
JIŘÍ GRUŠA, *The Questionnaire.*
MELA HARTWIG, *Am I a Redundant*
Human Being?
JOHN HAWKES, *The Passion Artist.*
Whistlejacket.
ELIZABETH HEIGHWAY, ED., *Contemporary*
Georgian Fiction.
ALEKSANDAR HEMON, ED.,
Best European Fiction.
AIDAN HIGGINS, *Balcony of Europe.*
Blind Man's Bluff
Bornholm Night-Ferry.
Flotsam and Jetsam.
Langrishe, Go Down.
Scenes from a Receding Past.
KEIZO HINO, *Isle of Dreams.*
KAZUSHI HOSAKA, *Plainsong.*
ALDOUS HUXLEY, *Antic Hay.*
Crome Yellow.
Point Counter Point.
Those Barren Leaves.
Time Must Have a Stop.
NAOYUKI II, *The Shadow of a Blue Cat.*
GERT JONKE, *The Distant Sound.*
Geometric Regional Novel.
Homage to Czerny.
The System of Vienna.
JACQUES JOUET, *Mountain R.*
Savage.
Upstaged.
MIEKO KANAI, *The Word Book.*
YORAM KANIUK, *Life on Sandpaper.*
HUGH KENNER, *Flaubert.*
Joyce and Beckett: The Stoic Comedians.
Joyce's Voices.
DANILO KIŠ, *The Attic.*
Garden, Ashes.
The Lute and the Scars
Psalm 44.
A Tomb for Boris Davidovich.
ANITA KONKKA, *A Fool's Paradise.*
GEORGE KONRÁD, *The City Builder.*
TADEUSZ KONWICKI, *A Minor Apocalypse.*
The Polish Complex.
MENIS KOUMANDAREAS, *Koula.*
ELAINE KRAF, *The Princess of 72nd Street.*
JIM KRUSOE, *Iceland.*
AYŞE KULIN, *Farewell: A Mansion in*
Occupied Istanbul.
EMILIO LASCANO TEGUI, *On Elegance*
While Sleeping.
ERIC LAURRENT, *Do Not Touch.*
VIOLETTE LEDUC, *La Bâtarde.*
EDOUARD LEVÉ, *Autoportrait.*
Suicide.
MARIO LEVI, *Istanbul Was a Fairy Tale.*
DEBORAH LEVY, *Billy and Girl.*
JOSÉ LEZAMA LIMA, *Paradiso.*
ROSA LIKSOM, *Dark Paradise.*
OSMAN LINS, *Avalovara.*
The Queen of the Prisons of Greece.
ALF MAC LOCHLAINN,
The Corpus in the Library.
Out of Focus.
RON LOEWINSOHN, *Magnetic Field(s).*
MINA LOY, *Stories and Essays of Mina Loy.*

D. KEITH MANO, *Take Five.*
MICHELINE AHARONIAN MARCOM,
The Mirror in the Well.
BEN MARCUS,
The Age of Wire and String.
WALLACE MARKFIELD,
Teitlebaum's Window.
To an Early Grave.
DAVID MARKSON, *Reader's Block.*
Wittgenstein's Mistress.
CAROLE MASO, *AVA.*
LADISLAV MATEJKA AND KRYSTYNA
POMORSKA, EDS.,
Readings in Russian Poetics:
Formalist and Structuralist Views.
HARRY MATHEWS, *Cigarettes.*
The Conversions.
The Human Country: New and
Collected Stories.
The Journalist.
My Life in CIA.
Singular Pleasures.
The Sinking of the Odradek
Stadium.
Tlooth.
JOSEPH MCELROY,
Night Soul and Other Stories.
ABDELWAHAB MEDDEB, *Talismano.*
GERHARD MEIER, *Isle of the Dead.*
HERMAN MELVILLE, *The Confidence-Man.*
AMANDA MICHALOPOULOU, *I'd Like.*
STEVEN MILLHAUSER, *The Barnum Museum.*
In the Penny Arcade.
RALPH J. MILLS, JR., *Essays on Poetry.*
MOMUS, *The Book of Jokes.*
CHRISTINE MONTALBETTI, *The Origin of Man.*
Western.
OLIVE MOORE, *Spleen.*
NICHOLAS MOSLEY, *Accident.*
Assassins.
Catastrophe Practice.
Experience and Religion.
A Garden of Trees.
Hopeful Monsters.
Imago Bird.
Impossible Object.
Inventing God.
Judith.
Look at the Dark.
Natalie Natalia.
Serpent.
Time at War.
WARREN MOTTE,
Fables of the Novel: French Fiction
since 1990.
Fiction Now: The French Novel in
the 21st Century.
Oulipo: A Primer of Potential
Literature.
GERALD MURNANE, *Barley Patch.*
Inland.
YVES NAVARRE, *Our Share of Time.*
Sweet Tooth.
DOROTHY NELSON, *In Night's City.*
Tar and Feathers.
ESHKOL NEVO, *Homesick.*
WILFRIDO D. NOLLEDO, *But for the Lovers.*
FLANN O'BRIEN, *At Swim-Two-Birds.*
The Best of Myles.
The Dalkey Archive.
The Hard Life.
The Poor Mouth.

FOR A FULL LIST OF PUBLICATIONS, VISIT:
www.dalkeyarchive.com

The Third Policeman.
CLAUDE OLLIER, *The Mise-en-Scène.*
Wert and the Life Without End.
GIOVANNI ORELLI, *Walaschek's Dream.*
PATRIK OUŘEDNÍK, *Europeana.*
The Opportune Moment, 1855.
BORIS PAHOR, *Necropolis.*
FERNANDO DEL PASO, *News from the Empire.*
Palinuro of Mexico.
ROBERT PINGET, *The Inquisitory.*
Mahu or The Material.
Trio.
MANUEL PUIG, *Betrayed by Rita Hayworth.*
The Buenos Aires Affair.
Heartbreak Tango.
RAYMOND QUENEAU, *The Last Days.*
Odile.
Pierrot Mon Ami.
Saint Glinglin.
ANN QUIN, *Berg.*
Passages.
Three.
Tripticks.
ISHMAEL REED, *The Free-Lance Pallbearers.*
The Last Days of Louisiana Red.
Ishmael Reed: The Plays.
Juice!
Reckless Eyeballing.
The Terrible Threes.
The Terrible Twos.
Yellow Back Radio Broke-Down.
JASIA REICHARDT, *15 Journeys Warsaw to London.*
NOËLLE REVAZ, *With the Animals.*
JOÃO UBALDO RIBEIRO, *House of the Fortunate Buddhas.*
JEAN RICARDOU, *Place Names.*
RAINER MARIA RILKE, *The Notebooks of Malte Laurids Brigge.*
JULIÁN RÍOS, *The House of Ulysses.*
Larva: A Midsummer Night's Babel.
Poundemonium.
Procession of Shadows.
AUGUSTO ROA BASTOS, *I the Supreme.*
DANIËL ROBBERECHTS, *Arriving in Avignon.*
JEAN ROLIN, *The Explosion of the Radiator Hose.*
OLIVIER ROLIN, *Hotel Crystal.*
ALIX CLEO ROUBAUD, *Alix's Journal.*
JACQUES ROUBAUD, *The Form of a City Changes Faster, Alas, Than the Human Heart.*
The Great Fire of London.
Hortense in Exile.
Hortense Is Abducted.
The Loop.
Mathematics:
The Plurality of Worlds of Lewis.
The Princess Hoppy.
Some Thing Black.
RAYMOND ROUSSEL, *Impressions of Africa.*
VEDRANA RUDAN, *Night.*
STIG SÆTERBAKKEN, *Siamese.*
Self Control.
LYDIE SALVAYRE, *The Company of Ghosts.*
The Lecture.
The Power of Flies.
LUIS RAFAEL SÁNCHEZ, *Macho Camacho's Beat.*
SEVERO SARDUY, *Cobra & Maitreya.*

NATHALIE SARRAUTE,
Do You Hear Them?
Martereau.
The Planetarium.
ARNO SCHMIDT, *Collected Novellas.*
Collected Stories.
Nobodaddy's Children.
Two Novels.
ASAF SCHURR, *Motti.*
GAIL SCOTT, *My Paris.*
DAMION SEARLS, *What We Were Doing and Where We Were Going.*
JUNE AKERS SEESE,
Is This What Other Women Feel Too?
What Waiting Really Means.
BERNARD SHARE, *Inish.*
Transit.
VIKTOR SHKLOVSKY, *Bowstring.*
Knight's Move.
A Sentimental Journey: Memoirs 1917–1922.
Energy of Delusion: A Book on Plot.
Literature and Cinematography.
Theory of Prose.
Third Factory.
Zoo, or Letters Not about Love.
PIERRE SINIAC, *The Collaborators.*
KJERSTI A. SKOMSVOLD, *The Faster I Walk, the Smaller I Am.*
JOSEF ŠKVORECKÝ, *The Engineer of Human Souls.*
GILBERT SORRENTINO,
Aberration of Starlight.
Blue Pastoral.
Crystal Vision.
Imaginative Qualities of Actual Things.
Mulligan Stew.
Pack of Lies.
Red the Fiend.
The Sky Changes.
Something Said.
Splendide-Hôtel.
Steelwork.
Under the Shadow.
W. M. SPACKMAN, *The Complete Fiction.*
ANDRZEJ STASIUK, *Dukla.*
Fado.
GERTRUDE STEIN, *The Making of Americans.*
A Novel of Thank You.
LARS SVENDSEN, *A Philosophy of Evil.*
PIOTR SZEWC, *Annihilation.*
GONÇALO M. TAVARES, *Jerusalem.*
Joseph Walser's Machine.
Learning to Pray in the Age of Technique.
LUCIAN DAN TEODOROVICI,
Our Circus Presents . . .
NIKANOR TERATOLOGEN, *Assisted Living.*
STEFAN THEMERSON, *Hobson's Island.*
The Mystery of the Sardine.
Tom Harris.
TAEKO TOMIOKA, *Building Waves.*
JOHN TOOMEY, *Sleepwalker.*
JEAN-PHILIPPE TOUSSAINT, *The Bathroom.*
Camera.
Monsieur.
Reticence.
Running Away.
Self-Portrait Abroad.
Television.
The Truth about Marie.